2014 Rainbow Award as Best Transgender Fiction

Moss gives young trans readers the benefit of a trans hero they can identify with and who overcomes tragedies unrelated to being rejected by family or being revealed as an "imposter." And he does the genre a great favor by writing a trans character so authentically from the core of his own experiences—one whose inner questions about his gender do not overwhelm the narrative, and who spends the majority of the book living and growing as a whole self: a future husband and father, a loyal son, a just employer, and a defender of innocent bystanders.

—Lambda Literary

Christopher Moss's *Beloved Pilgrim* is a wonder. Every now and then you stumble across a story that not only had to be told, but managed to get itself told by an accomplished author. *Beloved Pilgrim* is such a story. Thank you Mr. Moss. I am richer for the gift of your plainly beautiful words.

—Elisa's Reviews and Ramblings

By CHRISTOPHER HAWTHORNE MOSS

Beloved Pilgrim
A Fine Bromance

Published by HARMONY INK PRESS
www.harmonyinkpress.com

A FINE
BROMANCE

CHRISTOPHER
HAWTHORNE MOSS

DREAMSPINNER
PRESS

Published by
HARMONY INK PRESS

5032 Capital Circle SW, Suite 2, PMB# 279, Tallahassee, FL 32305-7886 USA
publisher@harmonyinkpress.com • harmonyinkpress.com

This is a work of fiction. Names, characters, places, and incidents either are
the product of author imagination or are used fictitiously, and any resemblance
to actual persons, living or dead, business establishments, events, or locales is
entirely coincidental.

A Fine Bromance
© 2016 Christopher Hawthorne Moss.

Cover Art
© 2016 AngstyG.
www.angstyg.com
Cover content is for illustrative purposes only and any person depicted on the
cover is a model.

All rights reserved. This book is licensed to the original purchaser only.
Duplication or distribution via any means is illegal and a violation of international
copyright law, subject to criminal prosecution and upon conviction, fines, and/
or imprisonment. Any eBook format cannot be legally loaned or given to others.
No part of this book may be reproduced or transmitted in any form or by any
means, electronic or mechanical, including photocopying, recording, or by any
information storage and retrieval system, without the written permission of the
Publisher, except where permitted by law. To request permission and all other
inquiries, contact Harmony Ink Press, 5032 Capital Circle SW, Suite 2, PMB#
279, Tallahassee, FL 32305-7886, USA, or publisher@harmonyinkpress.com.

ISBN: 978-1-63477-001-9
Digital ISBN: 978-1-63477-002-6
Library of Congress Control Number: 2016901425
Published August 2016
v. 1.0

Printed in the United States of America
∞
This paper meets the requirements of
ANSI/NISO Z39.48-1992 (Permanence of Paper).

This novel is dedicated to all the young and old who brave society's definitions of gender and create their own identities, in particular my friend Sean Bailey Czerwinski who made the Seattle papers with his decision to be the boy, and man, he knew he was. I also dedicate the novel to Aidan Key, who runs a major transgender organization in Washington State and has done pioneering work with both children and adults helping us all be our real selves. I happen to be one of the adults.

And as always, to my beloved Jim.

CHAPTER 1

"ROBBY, C'MON! Let someone else use the bathroom!" Robby's sister, Claire, shouted on the morning of the first day of school, her first day as a junior. And Robby's as a senior. Robby Czerwinski wiped the steam off the mirror and stared at what little he could see, not at all satisfied with the small image.

"Chill! I'm coming out," he called through the bathroom door. He reached for his robe and pulled it on, then opened the door before he tied the sash.

"*Eww*, Robby, cover yourself!" Claire complained as she pushed past him to go into the steamy bathroom to start her morning ritual.

Robby headed for his bedroom but remembered Claire had a full-length mirror in hers. He detoured into her room, since, with the sound of the shower coming on, he knew he could get a good look before she caught him.

He opened her door, then shut it quietly behind him, shaking his head at the table with the lighted mirror and a pile of cosmetics and the clothing strewn all over the bed and other furniture. He opened her closet door, and ignoring the scatter of shoes inside hanging half off the wire shoe rack, Robby took her sweaters off the hook over the mirror so he could get a full look at his body. What he saw in the mirror pleased him—a tall, slightly freckled boy with dark auburn hair cut short but not too short. Broad shoulders were wider than his hips. Best of all, his abs almost had a washboard definition to them. It almost made up for the slight underbite that made his jaw a bit weak.

But it was a buff boy he saw looking back at him. He had started working out in the late spring and really pushed himself all summer to get toned, his muscles defined. He almost couldn't recognize the broadly grinning kid in the mirror, holding his robe open in front. *If this doesn't do the trick, nothing will.*

He glanced down to the junction of his thighs. His dick dangled there, coming out from the small thatch of curly hair. "You're all manly muscle now, buddy," he said to it. "Start working like you're supposed to." His dick didn't answer him. He sighed. "At least start thinking about it, okay, bro?"

He gave himself a sardonic smile, then closed and tied his robe. *Patience*, he advised himself. He walked out of Claire's room and, hearing the shower shut off, ducked into his own to get dressed for school.

Though if getting buff doesn't work, he thought as he dressed, *I don't know what will.* No matter what he did, from looking at porn to handling himself down there, he couldn't get his brain to cooperate with the rest of him. Oh, he got hard if he played with himself, and he could bring himself off, but he just couldn't respond to the sight of a sexy woman's body. He looked at the pictures, but no matter how suggestive they were, they did nothing for him.

It's not that I'm gay—at least, I'm pretty sure I'm not. A few months ago he'd gone into a porn store, trying to look older, and while the clerk gave him the occasional suspicious look, he ultimately let him buy a gay sex magazine. He brought it home, locked his bedroom door, and looked at the pictures one by one. Nothing. Nada. Not a single stirring.

What's wrong with me? He knew from the way they talked that other boys found girls tantalizing in the extreme, but though the touch of his hand could get him started, he found himself focused on that feeling and never pictured a single partner, female or male. *I just don't understand. Doesn't one go with the other?*

There was no way he could talk to his mother about this, and he was mortified at the thought of talking about his "problem" with his friends, Luis and Max. They would either be so embarrassed they'd stop talking to him, or they'd tease him endlessly. So last semester he had gingerly approached his gym coach, Mr. Monroe, and explained about his lack of response to girls.

The usually gruff man looked uncomfortable. "Well, boy, do you think... you could... uh... be... gay?"

Robbie shrugged. Mr. Monroe didn't need to know about his experiment with gay porn. "I don't think so."

"Well, maybe you should talk with your dad about it."

Robby's dad was long out of the picture, but he didn't tell Mr. Monroe that. His dad hadn't stayed in touch with either him or Claire. Truth be told, Robby was afraid the coach would blame his problem on an absent father figure. He and his sister Claire had a running joke about that sort of armchair psychology, whether at school or elsewhere. The two would privately put their hands up and make them "talk," mouthing "Blah blah blah... your dad... blah blah blah," and laugh. He'd thanked Mr. Monroe and never mentioned it again.

At one point he happened to ride his bike along the street past the local Catholic church his mother still attended. Church was fast becoming irrelevant to him as he grew into his adolescent years, but after some second thoughts, Robby decided to approach the priest. He was with his friend Max, so he waited and went a few days later.

Father Martin asked him the same question as the coach about whether or not he was gay.

"I don't get turned on by boys or girls," he explained, his cheeks burning.

The priest looked doubtful and then asked, "Son, might you have a calling to the priesthood? Have you considered entering a seminary?"

Robby could definitely answer that question. "No, sir, I don't think so."

"Turn your troubles to God and pray for guidance," Father Martin suggested.

Robby politely agreed and left the confessional.

He spent some weeks trying not to think about his confusion. He let school distract him. He was in Quiz Kids, a sort of academic competition, now and studied a great deal. None of his friends participated in that one, but he palled around with a couple of the others, and it was only when one of the boys started to ask him about dating and telling Robby about his own attempts at attracting a girl that he had to put the emphasis back on his sexuality again. He realized that putting the boys off and making things up to sound knowledgeable was not going to hack it.

Finally he went to the high school psychologist, Mrs. French. He and Claire went to Highlands View High School in an eastern suburb of Seattle. That part of the world was known for its with-it school staff, fully aware of bullying due to orientation, race, you name it. But all the counselor said was, "Robby, you're probably just a late bloomer. You need to wait, to be open to your own body's needs. You need to think about what might be blocking your response. If your disinterest persists, then talk to me again if you come to any conclusions." He decided she was probably closest to being right, though nothing had come to him yet.

So he'd decided to work on his body. He thought if he ate right, slept plenty, drank lots of water, and worked out and got himself a more masculine physique, maybe whatever was slowing things down would clear up.

But it didn't. He was a senior now, and he was no closer to understanding his lack of sexual response than he had as a skinny nerd.

Robby sighed. If he didn't come to any conclusions now that he was about to turn eighteen, make the wrestling team, meet more mature girls, and finish high school, he would… well, he would think about that later.

Otherwise, he knew in the back of his mind, he would be off to college next fall, be expected to find a girl—or a boy—to date, get engaged, and then married. How could he do that, given his lack of interest in, well, anyone?

He slipped on his Nikes and tied them, then stood up to go to breakfast.

After wolfing down a bowl of cereal, he waited for Claire, who would drive him to school in the car they theoretically owned together. She used it more, being more social—or rather, more manipulative and selfish—but she knew she had to give him a ride, so she pouted and got behind the wheel. He knew better than to suggest he drive. Claire wouldn't stand for it.

As Claire sped up to go through yellow lights and took corners too fast, she asked Robby, "So now that you're such a big jock, are you going out for a sport?"

"Yeah, I'm thinking about trying out for the wrestling team."

She brightened. "Oh yeah? Cool. No more Mr. Brainiac? No more Quiz Kids?"

He glared at her. "No, I'll still do the Quiz Kids. Your brain is a muscle too, you know."

"Yeah, right," she said.

Once at the high school, she mumbled "Later" as she pulled into a student parking spot where she and Robby climbed out of the car. "What time do you need me to take you home?" she asked, turning back after a few steps toward the school entrance.

He took off his backpack, unzipped it, and rooted inside for the class schedule he had been mailed, along with every other kid in the school. "Let me see. It looks like my last period gets out at ten to three. But I may walk home with some of my friends."

"Fine with me," she called as she walked away.

Robby looked around to see if any of his friends were there yet. He spotted Luis moving along the main sidewalk with his forearm crutches. Luis had some sort of palsy or something. He wouldn't talk about it, but his legs were skinny and a little twisted, and he moved along using "Canadian crutches" as he called them. "Hey, Ramirez!" Robby called out, dashing to join him.

"Robby, dude!" he called, turning to meet him. "¿Qué pasa? Hey, look at you. You're all tough-looking!"

Robby shrugged. "I worked out this summer."

"There some *chica* you're looking to date?"

He shrugged again in response to Luis's leering expression. "Maybe."

"Lookin' good, bro…. Max better look out. You'll kick his butt."

Just as Luis said the name, the other boy walked up, high-fived Robby, and nodded to Luis. "Who's gonna kick my butt?" he asked.

Luis indicated Robby with a tilt of his head. "Hey, Nielsen. Robby's been buffing up."

Max, a brown-eyed boy with short black hair, checked Robby out. "Man, you look good. You work out or something, bro?"

Luis smirked. "Gonna ask Rob for a date, Max?"

Max gave him a dirty look and turned back to Robby. "You going to try out for something?"

Robby shrugged again. "Maybe wrestling."

Luis called their attention to another boy who was walking by. "Who's the new guy?"

Robby and Max turned to where Luis was looking. They saw a short boy wearing a jacket from an Olympia high school coming up the walk, glancing from side to side and blushing slightly.

Max said, "Huh. Is that a boy or a girl?"

Robby looked hard at Max. "Don't be stupid. It's a boy. Can't you see how he wears his hair? And look how he walks." But truth be told, Robby had to spy on the new boy out of the corner of his eye to be certain. He looked like a boy, dressed like one, had a very short haircut, but his hands and feet were small. He was also short like Robby.

Max stepped forward as the boy came alongside them. "Dude," he greeted. "You new here?"

The boy looked up sharply and gave them a nervous smile. "Yeah, my dad got a job at Microsoft, so we moved here. I'm Andy Kahn. I'm a senior."

Robby, Luis, and Max introduced themselves and reached to grip the new boy's right hand in a variety of salutes.

Luis said, "Bummer to have to switch schools with only one year to go."

Robby added, "But Highlands View is a good school. You'll like it here."

Andy smiled again, nodded, and made positive noises. "Nice to meet you all. So we're all seniors." He glanced down at his clothing and asked, "So, any of you on a team?"

Luis laughed. "Depends." Andy gave him a blank look.

"He means if you're talking about sports, maybe," Max explained. "But Robby here is on the Quiz Kids team, unless he's too buff for that now."

Andy interjected, "Quiz Kids? What's that?"

Robby gave him a sheepish look. "Quiz Kids. You know, like High School Bowl. An academic competition club. You answer questions about history and math and stuff."

Much to Robby's surprise, Andy's tense look cleared. "Oh yeah? That sounds great. Do you have any openings?"

Robby glanced between Luis and Max. "See? It's not just me." He looked back at Andy. "Yeah, I'm sure you can try out. What are your subjects?"

Andy acted as if he couldn't talk fast enough. "I really like history and other social sciences. Also German. You?" he asked.

"Math and science mostly. We can use a good social-science contestant. Let me talk to the coach about you." He grinned. "You should meet my aunt."

Looking uncertain, Andy asked, "Your aunt?"

Luis laughed again. "She's ancient history all right. Kind of a nut." He tried to duck as Robby threw a feint at him.

"She collects things. She was head of the history department at a Catholic school. She's got books and pictures and knickknacks and you name it. All over her house. She lives near here. I could introduce you."

Andy smiled uncertainly. "Cool, dude," he said.

The bell rang for school to start, and the four boys headed off in their individual directions. Robby noticed Andy pull out his schedule and peer at it in a panic. "If you want, I can show you where your homeroom is."

"Thanks, man," Andy said, sounding relieved.

AS THEY walked down the hall, Andy glanced at the other boy. *He's reading me as a boy. That is so great.*

He wondered what his new friend would think if he knew Andy wasn't a boy in the traditional sense. He'd been born Andrea Ruth Kahn and grown up unhappily wearing dresses and skirts, though as little as possible. After years of not understanding why he was so dissatisfied with his body, why he felt like a freak, he had finally found a book at the city library about people who were transgender. It made lights go off all over his brain.

It had taken a lot of courage for Andrea—Andy—to tell his mother. She hadn't understood what he was saying at first, until he loaned her the book he'd found. After that, he could practically hear the gears in her brain working. His father asked to speak with him one evening, and the two of them had had a good heart-to-heart. They finally had a family conference with Gabe, his younger brother, and started to talk about Andy in male pronouns. His mother took over and got him counseling and boy's clothing, from underwear to a winter jacket, and went with him to the doctor to talk about getting onto hormones.

8

Andy knew how lucky he was. His parents didn't think he was nuts or a pervert or just being difficult. They listened, they asked questions, and, ultimately, they not only accepted him but supported him. They even said they would support any surgery he wanted and the doctor would agree to do. His mother's eyes flashed when she said, "And if they won't do it, we'll find one who will!"

His brother, Gabe, was the best. Andy's revelation hadn't fazed him in the least. Gabe's reaction was just to say "I knew it all along. You've always seemed more like a big brother than a big sister to me."

Andy's relief and gratitude knew no bounds.

He'd told his parents he wanted a fresh start, somewhere where none of the other kids had known him as Andrea. His father, who had worked for the State of Washington, found a good job at Microsoft, and they moved to the Eastside. They contacted the school district administrator and got an appointment with one of the counselors. His mother and father had both come with him to the new school. Andy's mom marched into the appointment ready for a fight, but all of them, including Andy, had been gratified at how well-informed the woman had been and how aware of the needs he would have as a transgender student.

"You aren't the first transgender student in the district," Mrs. French said. "You will be the first as far as we know at Highlands View, though. We had a transgender girl at one of the other high schools. She managed to pass quite well, and no one was ever the wiser. We'll have to determine how to deal with bathrooms and showers for gym class, but we'll have it all in place before school starts."

They left the administration office elated, and Andy's smile about split his face.

During the summer Andy went on hormones to begin his development as a male and had a hysterectomy. The school administrators had decided Andy would use the boys' bathrooms and would be excused from showering. He knew there would be questions from the other students about that, but he figured he would handle those when they came up.

Robby pointed Andy in the direction of his homeroom, and before they parted, they exchanged phone numbers and e-mail addresses so they could get in touch about the next meeting of Quiz Kids. "It sure was lucky running into you guys so quickly. You make me feel like I've moved to a good school," Andy said. Robby put out his hand, and they did a fist-bump handshake.

CHAPTER 2

BIOLOGY CLASS was starting when Andy finally found the classroom on the second floor. The teacher, a thin gray-haired woman with a predatory glare, barely registered his intrusion. Andy looked for a vacant seat, and to his pleased surprise found one right next to Robby. He made his way to it, climbed on the stool at the raised table, and nodded when Robby passed him the textbook from a pile near him. He mouthed "Thanks" and turned his attention to the teacher, who was speaking.

"We won't be doing much dissecting this year as the emphasis will be on sexuality and genetics. Everything from worms and fruit flies to human biology and genetic diseases. The textbook will prove useful some of the time, but it is, of course, already out of date, so I will be directing you to websites and handouts for the latest topics." The woman scanned the room. "You all have access to the Internet, I assume?"

It happened that a few of the students did not. The teacher shook her head and replied, "Well, you'll have to find a way to access the material I assign you. If you don't have access yourself, you can use the library's computers or even the computer lab here at the school. But I am willing to talk to your parents or guardian about the importance of teenagers having access to the Internet. Just let me know."

After class was dismissed, Andy turned to Robby and said, "Hey, bro, good to see you again. I didn't catch the teacher's name. I suppose it's on my class assignment list...."

He looked through the pile of papers he was carrying, but Robby beat him to it. "Mrs. Pollack," he said.

Max, who Andy hadn't noticed sitting in the back of the room, came up behind him and said, "Poll-ock." Then he smirked and slapped Robby on the back. "Mrs. Poll-ock."

Andy gave him a disdainful look.

"Don't mind Max. He's an idiot. He's on the wrestling team," Robby said, as if that explained everything.

Andy nodded.

Max asked him, "You going out for a sport, Andy? You look like a... well... a chess club member."

Rolling his eyes, Andy breathed, "A comedian. Lucky us."

Max and Robby exchanged raised eyebrows as they each put their books under one arm and started to walk toward the door. Andy tried to carry his books the same way but had trouble balancing them. He hoped he would get the knack soon.

The trio passed into the corridor. It was full of students streaming both ways, others gathering by lockers, and still others peering at the small number plates over the classroom doors. "Wait a minute," Andy said, then consulted his class schedule. "English next, in Room 201." He looked toward the stairs. "This way."

Max made a limp-wristed gesture. "Oh, Mithter Foxth. Lucky you."

Glaring at Max, Andy and Robby both shook their heads. "Oh, Max, you're such a dick," Robby said.

"What's with the gay bashing, Max? You sweet on the man or something?" Andy quipped, feeling like he'd scored one off the bigot.

"Really, Max. It's the twenty-first century, you know. Get with the program." Robby looked at Andy, clearly embarrassed by Max's comment. "I hope you don't think we're all like Max," he said.

Andy shook his head. "Glad to hear it."

Max, who seemed embarrassed by his own bad behavior, muttered something about having to see a man about a dog and took off down the corridor.

"What a jerk," Andy said.

Robby looked after Max's departing back. "Yeah, he can be. But he's just testing the water. I actually think he might be gay himself. He drops a lot of hints. But who knows."

Taking another look at his class schedule, Andy said, "Well, maybe I'll see you at lunch or something. I gotta go."

Glancing over Andy's shoulder, Robby said, "Yeah, you have the same lunch period I do. See you later." He made an *okay* gesture with his hand and headed off in the other direction.

THREE PERIODS later Robby saw Andy in the lunch line. He waited for Andy to get to the till and pay and then called him over to the table where he sat. This time Max wasn't present, just Luis and their friend Rhonda. He said, "Andy, you met Luis, and this is Rhonda."

Andy greeted Robby and Luis and then looked at Rhonda, who made a sour face.

"And you're another boy. Great," she grumbled, her almond-shaped eyes narrowing. She had that disgruntled look some heavyset girls got, something that puzzled Robby, who thought Rhonda looked just fine the way she was.

Robby and Luis laughed. Luis explained, "Rhonda is the school lesbian. Don't take it personally."

Rhonda gave him an irritated look. "I never said I was a lesbian. I'm just a strong feminist."

13

"Good for you. Me too," Andy replied, reaching to shake Rhonda's hand. "Good to meet you, sister," he said.

Rhonda eyed him but didn't reply.

"So how was English?" Robby asked.

Andy started to stuff french fries into his mouth. "Okay. We're gonna read this novel by some guy named Forster. *Maurice* or something. Maybe Max is right about the teacher. It's about a boy in some English school who's sweet on another boy."

"I heard of that book. They made a movie too. I think Hugh Grant is in it." Rhonda started eating her meatballs. "Yuck, these are terrible. What did they make them out of, dog meat?"

"I'll eat them," Robby said, taking Rhonda's plate and using a fork to push the meatballs onto his own. He already had a ham sandwich on it, half-eaten.

"Suit yourself," Rhonda said. She started to get up and gather her things. "Well, since I don't have anything to eat, I'll just go to the vending machines. Either of you want anything?"

Robby and Andy shook their heads. "No, thanks," they chorused, then looked at each other and laughed.

"You owe me a Coke," Andy said and started to count.

"Stop," said Robby.

They sat in silence for a couple of minutes, and then Robby asked Andy, "So why did you move up here from Olympia?"

Shrugging, Andy answered quickly. "My dad got a job at Microsoft."

Robby nodded sagely. "You into computer games?"

Andy shrugged again. "Not so much. I like computers fine. I just use them for other things."

"Me too," Robby said. "The games are all right, but everyone is so competitive. I just like to look around on Wikipedia, and I watch science and math videos online."

"He's a *brainiac*," Luis put in.

Robby blushed slightly. "Not really. A little, maybe. Not so you'd notice or anything."

Andy snorted. "Well, don't that just beat the Dutch."

"Beat… the Dutch?" Robby asked. "I don't get it."

Andy looked surprised he had said that phrase. "Uh, it's an old expression, from the Civil War. I don't know what it means. It just means—well—you know."

Robby nodded. "Yeah."

The two boys each colored a little. Then they both laughed.

"Guess I'm the history buff," Andy said sarcastically.

AFTER SCHOOL Robby got home to an empty house. His mom was still at work, but he didn't know why his sister was gone. He went to the kitchen to look for something to eat. The fridge was mostly empty. His sister was always starving herself. His mom tended to bring home takeout. He saw a small container near the back of the top shelf and reached for it. When he opened it, he couldn't identify what it had been. It smelled rancid. He tossed it in the trash and looked in the cupboards. He found a little cellophane-wrapped package of saltine crackers and ate them, stale as they were.

He heard the front door open and crash closed. "Claire?" he called.

His sister poked her head into the kitchen with a sort of euphoric look on her face, like she had just left a royal ball or something. "Oh hey, Bob," she said.

He cringed. He hated being called Bob.

"Hey, did you see that new kid at school today? Annie or Abby or something? Deedee says she's a dyke. I heard she had to have some special arrangements for using the boys' shower in gym class."

Before Robby could reply, she had gone. He heard her steps on the stairs running up to the level where their rooms were. He thought to himself, *Dyke named Annie or Abby?* No, he hadn't met any girls like that. Surely Rhonda would've said if there was a new lesbian in class. He kept nibbling on the crackers.

The telephone rang, and Robby reached for it where it hung on the wall. "Hello?"

"Robby? Is that Robby?" The voice on the other end was shaky, elderly.

"Hello, Aunt Ivy. Yes, this is Robby."

Ivy was Robby's eighty-year-old great-aunt, and he was exceedingly fond of her. She was his mother's great-aunt, actually, and rather frail and nervous. She lived in the area, maybe a twenty-minute drive from his house.

"Oh, Robby, I'm so glad it's you."

"What's wrong, Aunt Ivy? You sound upset." Robby leaned back against the kitchen counter and listened carefully to her faint voice.

"It's the captain. I can't find him. You didn't come over and take him, did you?"

Robby thought hard. *The captain? What captain?*

"I don't know what captain you mean, Aunt Ivy," he said.

He heard her moan, a thin, warbling sound. "Oh, you know. The captain. The medallion I had of a captain in the navy. I can't remember his name."

That captain! His great-aunt collected all types of memorabilia—figurines, ceramics, jewelry, funny sketches, silverware, snow globes, state crest bells, you name it. He remembered the captain now, a small brass medallion of a man in a captain's hat, a captain's uniform, and with a big white moustache, just his head looking right. On the other side were some words saying it was the anniversary of some ship launch.

"Oh yes, the captain. I know just the one you mean. What do you mean he's missing?"

Aunt Ivy sounded a little calmer when she responded. "Yes, the captain of the *Houston*. He's just gone. I had him this morning,

I think it was, or maybe it was yesterday morning. Right here on the mantel. Now there is just a blank space where he was."

Robby put a finger to his lips, thinking. "Could you have moved it?"

"Him."

Robby stopped and asked, "Aunt Ivy?"

She cleared her throat. "You said 'it.' He's a 'him.'"

His eyebrows went up at the correction. "Yes, of course. Him. Could you have moved him?"

Robby heard a meow in the background behind Ivy's voice. He knew it was her cat, a big orange tom named Mr. Duck. "The Duck wants your attention."

Ivy muttered, "He just wants treats. Now why would I move a thing, dear? This is where he belongs. On the mantel with the model of the ship. Near the glass paperweight of the ship's wheel. And the commemorative coins of the ships of the line from the Royal Navy. And my little miniature of Admiral William Brown, that Irishman who fought for the Argentines."

Robby smiled. His aunt, for all her apparent doddering ways, was sharp as a tack. If he had a fondness for history, it was thanks to her and her massive collection of historically significant artifacts. Many an afternoon and evening he had spent with her, going through her collection. She would lift one from its place of honor and show it to him. He would take it in his hand and admire it while Aunt Ivy told him all about it, what it was, where it came from, and what historical significance it held. He wished he could remember the name of the ship captain on the medallion.

"Captain Albert H. Rooks," Ivy said. She had a way of making Robby feel like she could read his mind. "You remember. He commanded the *Houston* in the Southeast Asian theater in World War II. He went down with his ship in 1942. The medallion was commissioned when he received a posthumous award of honor."

Robby mimed a kiss at the receiver of the telephone. Dear Aunt Ivy.

"Do you want me to come over and help you look for it?" he asked.

There was a pause, and then the old woman said, "Not tonight, dear. I have my ladies coming over. But how about tomorrow after school? You are still in high school, aren't you? About three thirty?"

"Let's make it four o'clock. That way I won't be late."

Her voice became shaky again. "Oh dear, I do hope you can help me find him. It's such a dear thing. And the captain was such a handsome man. I can't imagine what could have become of him."

Robby reassured her. "I'll come over tomorrow afternoon at four, and we'll look for it. If we have to turn heaven and earth, I'm sure we will find it."

"Well, I hope we don't have to do *that*. I will see you tomorrow, then. Good-bye." And she hung up the phone.

Smiling to himself, Robby thought about going to see his great-aunt. She would probably invite him to dinner. His mother and sister wouldn't mind. And like every meal he ever had at Ivy's house, it would be a Banquet frozen chicken pot pie. She loved those pot pies.

Robby sighed, picked up his books from the kitchen table, tucked them under his arm, and headed up the stairs to his room to study.

CHAPTER 3

"YOU THINK you got a zit?"

Andy, who had been examining his chin in the boys' restroom mirror, turned to see Robby at the sink next to him. "Hey, Robby, how ya doing? No, I just was checking to see if my beard is coming in yet."

Robby chuckled. He rinsed his hands, reached for a paper towel, and asked, "Is it on your schedule for today?"

Realizing he'd said something that might lead to difficult questions, Andy reddened. "Uh, no, I do this every day." He had been on testosterone injections for months now and expected them to result in some beard growth soon. But Robby didn't know about him being on T, nor should he, so his answer might have seemed odd.

"Aren't you kinda young for a beard?" Robby asked.

"I dunno. But I check. I do have some peach fuzz, and I shaved it so it will come in thicker." Andy made a mental note to train his mouth not to drop these hints about his transition. All that time spent on Facebook FTM groups must have gotten him too used to sharing. After combing the Internet for other transgender kids, Andy had found a couple of sites, one for FTM—female to male—trans kids and adults. It wasn't very active, but he'd found

19

a few guys who gave him their own take on social relationships. On Facebook he found more sites for guys like him—in school, basically wondering about the same things he was, but they exhibited some of the confidence he wanted to mirror.

"Yeah, well, whatever. I can grow a beard, sort of, but I don't want one. Not yet, anyway." Robby flashed Andy a broad grin.

"So what's the latest on your Aunt Ivy?" Andy asked as they walked toward the exit.

"It's really weird. First she couldn't find a medallion, then a deck of tarot cards went missing. I'm beginning to wonder if she has Alzheimer's or something."

"That sucks," Andy replied as he reached to push the door open. "Ow!"

The swinging door flew toward him and made his wrist snap backward. Three boys came into the bathroom, shoving Andy and Robby back into it.

"Well, look who we have here!" said the lead boy, who had on a black T-shirt with the Black Veil Brides logo on it. His hair was shaved on one side and spiky on the other. He had a chain attached to one earring and then to a stud in his lip. In spite of his slovenly appearance, he was obviously well-off, his clothes and jewelry of high quality. His two companions, both attired as he was but not so expensively, flanked him. One wore shades, the other an openmouthed dull look.

"It's the class freaks," said the first boy.

Robby scowled. "What do you want, Bradley?" He turned to Andy. "Bradley—better known as Smartass—Grease, and Smack."

The boy with the sunglasses, who was apparently Grease, shoved Andy hard in the shoulder. "Yeah, it's the girl boy."

"Or maybe it's the boy girl," Smack said, his dull expression not changing.

Andy eyed the boys cautiously, choosing not to engage them.

Smartass leveled his eyes on Robby. "You hangin' out with the freak now?" he asked. "I know you got all manly muscle, but why you want to hang out with this trannie?"

Robby frowned at the three punks. "Leave him alone."

The three boys looked at each other and crowed with laughter. "Him? Why you callin' her 'him'? Or don't you know?" He looked to his friends. "Let's show Robby what Andrea's got!"

The three boys reached for Andy, one grabbing his jacket shoulder, another dragging his pack from his opposite shoulder, and Smartass reaching for his belt.

Andy watched as Robby stepped forward and shoved Smartass back against the swinging door. "I told you to leave him alone."

The other two boys stepped back when their ringleader lost his grip on Andy's belt. They glared at Robby.

"What do you want with him, anyway? What's he ever done to you?" Robby stood with his hands on his hips, glaring at all three.

Smartass had some trouble regaining his balance as he hit the swinging door and almost fell backward through it. He righted himself and stood facing Robby and Andy with a sneer. "Guess your girlfriend hasn't shown you her pussy yet."

The door came swinging in, hitting Smartass on the back. Mr. Monroe, the gym coach, stood in the doorway. He was wearing shorts, as usual, his field jacket, a baseball cap with a *H* on it, and athletic shoes and socks. His hair could hardly be seen under the cap, it was so short and slate gray, contrasting with his dark skin. "What's going on in here?" he demanded. "Oh, it's you, Bradley." He glanced over and saw Andy, who was looking away.

Monroe asked, "He harassing you, Kahn?"

Robby answered "Yeah" just as Andy said "No big deal."

"What?" Robby asked incredulously. "The asshole was just about to pants you."

"It's nothing," Andy said in an irritated voice. "Just drop it."

21

Robby stared at him. "Why are you letting this jerk do this?"

"Just drop it," Andy pleaded, his voice going up in pitch. He cleared his throat. "It's nothing, Mr. Monroe," he said in his normal voice. "Just messin' around."

"You sure about this?" he asked Andy.

"Yeah," Andy said, still not meeting anyone's eyes.

Mr. Monroe turned to the three ruffians and said in a stern voice, "This school has a no-bullying policy. You know that."

The three boys stood with their arms at their sides, their eyes round and hurt, but with smiles tugging at the edges of their lips. "We weren't doin' nothin', Mr. Monroe. Honest." Smartass looked for confirmation from his confederates.

The other two boys chimed in.

"No way!

"We weren't bullying the little...."

Andy looked up, angry and hurt, when the boy called Grease let the comment fall away without adding some insulting word. "Let's go, Robby."

Robby looked at him and nodded. They walked around the gym teacher and pushed through the door, leaving the three bullies alone with the coach.

They walked down the corridor several feet before either spoke. Finally Robby said, "What the hell was that all about?"

Andy stopped in his tracks and glared at Robby, who stopped and faced him. "I said it was nothing!"

Robby backed up and raised an arm in a *whoa* position. "Okay, man, I'll drop it. But you gotta admit that was weird."

Andy dropped his chin to his chest. "I wish you'd just forget about it. It wasn't anything. They were just mouthin' off."

Robby stared at him a moment longer, then shrugged and turned down another hallway to his next class. Andy watched him go, still shaking inside and wondering how long it would take before Smartass and his friends let the whole school know he was trans.

Sitting in the school library with books about the Seven Years' War spread out on the table in front of him, Robby was lost in thought. He riffled through the pages of one book, not looking at it while he considered what had happened in the bathroom. He had sometimes been the object of bullying, for no reason other than that he seemed weak. *This is why I worked out all summer.* It was the first time he had ever defended anyone else, and it felt good. Mostly he simply didn't like Smartass and his buddies, but he also felt bad for Andy, who was new and short. He was puzzled by Andy's reaction, though. Instead of acting scared or defending himself, he just wanted it all glossed over. Why in the world would he react that way? Maybe he was too small to fight the boys, though Robby suspected if anyone stood up to them, they would back down. Even if they had fought, Andy and Robby could have gotten a few punches in. And why did Smartass say that thing about Andy's "pussy"? Boys didn't have pussies, but some other boys liked to joke that they did. It was part of the constant fag baiting that went on with boys. It was common to call each other "fag" or worse, even when no one was actually suggesting a boy was gay. It was just a way to put each other down. Robby was sensitive to some of the name-calling, given his puzzling lack of sexual interest in girls, or for that matter, boys. But he had made his peace with the name-calling, or thought he had.

But with bullies it was more threatening. It sure felt like that with the encounter in the boys' bathroom. Robby was about to shrug it all off when his eyes lit on two portraits in the book he was scanning.

The Chevalier d'Éon. He had heard of him. Of her. There was a Japanese anime character based on him—her. In the anime it was a girl who fought with a sword. But he seemed to remember that in real life the chevalier was a man who disguised himself as a woman to be a spy for the French crown. He looked at the two portraits.

One was of a man of aristocratic bearing from the mid-eighteenth century. The other was a woman of the same era, wearing a black-brimmed hat and a crucifix. They could be the same person, though the portraitists' styles were different enough to make the chin and nose and the fullness of face vary. He read with interest about how d'Éon had to dress as a woman in order to gain access to the Empress Elizabeth of Russia. She wound up serving the empress as a woman. Though d'Éon served in the dragoons upon his return to France, his life as a woman must have appealed to him, since he then claimed to have been born a girl and forced to live as a boy and then a man. At one point there was even a London Stock Exchange wager set up as to whether the chevalier was male or female. The mystery continued for some years, the chevalier claiming to have been born a woman but raised as a boy, even after the deaths of Louis XV and Louis XVI and the chevalier's being sent to debtor's prison in England. Upon his or her death at the age of eighty-one, a doctor testified that the chevalier was born biologically male.

Wow, this puts my sexual problems in perspective. Robby wondered if the situation with Andy was that he was transgender. It would explain a few things: his sister saying Andy was a lesbian, and the boys in the bathroom talking about a pussy. Plus Andy was so short and had small hands and feet. And he was concerned about whether he was growing a beard. None of this proved anything, but it would explain a few things.

Still, Robby had read enough about gender identity to understand it didn't matter what Andy had or did not have between his legs. What mattered was what Andy had between his ears. It was the gender of the brain that counted, not the body.

Robby decided that either way, it was none of his business and he would relate to Andy as Andy wanted.

WHEN HE saw Andy again, it all seemed to have blown over. Apparently Robby acted the way Andy wanted, for they went back to their old behavior. They joked around, called each other mild, inoffensive names, argued about current events, started practice for Quiz Kids, and hung out with their friends, just as they had before. Robby managed to hide that he occasionally watched Andy for signs, one way or another, and finally decided it didn't matter.

One day after school, Robby went to Great-aunt Ivy's house to discover that yet another knickknack was missing. This time it was a little porcelain snuffbox. Ivy was distraught over its loss. She explained to him that while the tarot card deck was just a reproduction of the original, with its images of Regency personalities and events, the little box was a genuine Limoges from the period of Louis-Napoleon, Emperor of France. This reminded Robby of the Chevalier d'Éon, and it didn't surprise him at all that his great-aunt knew all about her.

"There aren't that many stories of transgender women in history, not since the time of the Romans, but there have been many, many transgender men," she explained. "James Barry was a British surgeon who performed the first caesarean section where the mother and child both survived. They found out he was born a woman when the housekeeper found him dead in his parlor. Then there was Albert Cashier, one of perhaps over a hundred women who served as men in the Civil War on both sides, and who continued to live as a man until nearly her death. Or his death, I should say. It is surprisingly common."

She got up from the sofa and went to one of her many bookshelves, peered through the titles, and selected one. "I just got this a few weeks ago. It's *They Fought Like Demons*, about all the women who enlisted in the Union and Confederate armies. Some of them did it to be near husbands. Others took off the uniform and wore dresses for the rest of their lives. But there were plenty like Cashier who preferred to be recognized as men."

25

Taking the book from her hand, Robby riffled through it, looking at the photos and reading snippets. "I didn't realize there were so many transgender men out there."

Ivy nodded. "I was looking on some website the other day and found all these transgender people there. That means female to male transgender people. I can't help but wonder what old Albert Cashier and Chevalier d'Éon would have made of this. But they were very brave to live as they did when they did. It's not easy now, but it's a lot easier, at least in the western world."

Looking up where she stood near him, Robby nodded and was thoughtful. He wasn't going to tell his Aunt Ivy about Andy. That was Andy's business. But he couldn't help but wonder if Andy was transgender, as his great-aunt described it.

The missing items from her collection were starting to become noticeable. He had wondered if her memory was starting to go, but listening to her talk about history made him doubt it.

"Has anybody been in here, maybe looking around?" he asked her.

She looked at him, her eyes distant. "Lots of people. You've been here. The ladies from my groups. Your Uncle Roger. The cable man. The grocery delivery man. I have classes from the junior high come in sometimes to look at all my junk. And Mr. Duck and me." She leaned down to give the cat a scratch under his chin, where he rubbed against her leg. "He and I have been here." She looked straight into Robby's eyes. "You think someone might actually be coming in here and stealing the things? Like a burglar?"

Robby just sat and thought. He looked around the room, then got up and walked into the dining room. He moved from bookshelf to tables to windowsills, then on to the kitchen. Everywhere he went he touched things, not the items themselves but the surfaces where they lay or stood.

When he came back into the sitting room, his great-aunt Ivy was still where he had left her, standing by the sofa looking at him. "I don't know, Aunt Ivy. At first I thought you were starting to lose your memory, but I'm starting to realize you're as sharp as ever. If things are vanishing from their places, it's because someone is moving them. Or removing them. I just don't know who or why or if they just misplace them or take them or what. At least we know it's not ghosts."

There was a twinkle in Ivy's eyes as she said, "Why not ghosts?"

ROBBY SAW Andy at his locker and hailed him. "Hey, Andy, do you have to go straight home?" he asked.

Andy took out his phone and checked the calendar. "No, I don't. How come?"

"I want you to meet my great-aunt Ivy."

Andy just looked at him as he shoved books into his book bag. "Why?"

Robby looked at him. "What do you mean, why? She's interesting, and I want you to meet her. And you're interesting, and I want her to meet you. Besides, she has a mystery going on."

Andy opened his mouth as if to protest but stopped. "A mystery? What kind of mystery?"

Robby grinned. He knew he had Andy's attention. "She has this collection of all sorts of memorabilia. Hundreds of items. You know. I told you about all the ones that have gone missing. I used to think she was going loony, but now I think the things are really being stolen or something. I think if we put our three heads together, we might figure it out."

Andy nodded. "We could play Holmes and Watson." He grinned at Robby's rolled eyes. "Well, that's better than the Hardy Boys." He thought a moment and asked, "What do you think might be happening to it all? Is someone selling it for drug money? Or is it just a light-fingered squirrel?"

Robby looked at him. "You watch way too many movies."

"That's true. No mystery there." Andy pulled on his jacket. "Okay, you're on. How do we get there?"

"My sister, Claire, has the car and will drop us off."

Andy stopped in his tracks again. "Your sister Claire? The junior, right? I don't think she likes me."

He looked at Andy. "I doubt she knows you're alive. She's way self-absorbed."

Andy started walking again. "Okay, if you say so."

CHAPTER 4

"THAT'S FUNNY. She's usually here." Robby tried the doorknob, then knocked on the front door of Great-aunt Ivy's house.

"She leaves the door unlocked? No wonder things are going missing at her place," Andy replied.

The house was a two-story wood frame with a small but neat front yard. There were a couple of hydrangeas flanking the concrete steps, but of course they had no flowers in November. The welcome mat had two silhouettes of cats standing above the word *Welcome* and was immaculately clean and swept.

"Only when she's home." Robby knocked again. "Well, she's usually here, and I guess she figures no one will come in when she is. I know that doesn't make any sense, but this used to be a terribly safe residential neighborhood. It mostly still is." Robby peered through the tall narrow window to the left of the door. "I guess she's gone out." He fished the key ring from his pants pockets and selected one.

Andy fell back a bit. "She won't mind?"

As Robby unlocked and opened the door, he reassured him. "Naw, she's cool with it."

The moment they were inside the foyer of the little house, Andy's eyes widened in astonishment. "My God! Look at this place!"

He walked in, gazing all around. The house was immaculately clean and neat, but every square inch of space was covered with, if it wasn't carefully planned, total clutter. The foyer walls were lined with framed artwork, and the hall table had its own share of figurines and memorabilia. The floor, with a clear path through the middle, likewise had taller things, like an umbrella stand made of an elephant's foot and a black-faced statue of a man holding out a ring to tie up a horse.

"The really amazing thing about it all is that everything has some historical significance. The little guy is from some Southern politician's front yard. That first-day cover envelope"— Robby indicated a small frame just above the hall table on the wall—"commemorates the attack on New Orleans by the North in April 1862."

Andy leaned forward to see the stamp on the envelope that showed a row of different types of ships on fire at a New Orleans levee.

"Why is she so into history?" Andy inquired.

Robby took off his jacket and hung it on a coat tree that looked like it must have come from some nineteenth-century manor house. "She was a history teacher at St. Madeleine Sophie School in Bellevue for over fifty years."

Andy made an impressed noise in his throat. "I thought teachers didn't make much money. But all this stuff—it must have cost her a fortune."

They walked into the parlor, which was even more amazing than the foyer. "She was head of the department and also had quite a retirement fund, but she also had money from her parents and her husband. Plus the stuff is mostly not all that valuable, or so she tells me. I mean, the first-day cover was just from a few years ago. And the tarot cards were reproductions, not originals. Fact is, I don't know if she even knows which items are worth anything. Mostly they're just glorious junk."

"You can say that again," observed Andy.

Robby grinned. "Which? Glorious or junk?"

Giving him a sardonic smile, Andy replied, "Both."

While Andy went about the room examining every single item or group of items, Robby called for his aunt Ivy up the stairs that led to the second floor. He got no response and went to look in the dining room and kitchen. He came back and observed, "It's a good thing these Seattle-area houses don't usually have basements. Otherwise I would have had to go looking there too."

Andy stood by the fireplace mantel with something in his hand. "Didn't you say one of the things missing was a commemorative medallion of some World War II ship captain?"

He walked over to him and looked at what he held. "Oh yeah, Captain Rooks. This one turned up again. So did the tarot cards. Right back where she left them."

Andy stared at him and then carefully placed Captain Rooks as neatly as possible in the same spot he had found him. "Weeirrrd," he said. "So were you right? Is her memory just going?"

Robby put a finger to the medallion and moved it a few millimeters. "No, I saw myself that it was missing, and now it's back."

"And you don't think she did it herself?"

Looking thoughtful for a moment, Robby shook his head. "I don't know, but I don't think so." He shivered melodramatically. In a mock-Transylvanian accent, he said, "I'm beginning to think there are otherworldly spirits acting."

Andy laughed aloud. "Now wouldn't that be a hoot?" He was already looking around the room for some other treasure.

"Let me give you the tour." Andy followed Robby into the dining room with its exquisite chandelier. "That's from Errol Flynn's Hollywood house."

Andy quipped, "He died with a hard-on." The look on Robby's face made him realize he had made a tasteless joke. "You know, that movie, *They Died with Their Boots On*?"

Robby grinned sheepishly. "Cool! You're an old movie buff! My mom likes to watch TCM."

CHRISTOPHER HAWTHORNE MOSS

Andy's face cleared and he laughed. "Mine too. I heard that Flynn died 'in the saddle,' so to speak."

The two boys shared the moment of companionability and laughed together.

After Andy had looked around the dining room for a few minutes, Robby gestured toward the hallway. "C'mon, I'll show you the things upstairs."

They went to the foot of the stairs. Along the wall was a mismatched set of framed portraits, or reproductions, of American presidents. At the landing at the top of the stairs, Robby opened the nearest door. He led Andy into what was clearly an office.

Andy strolled in, no longer surprised by the memorabilia that plastered every surface. What did bring him up short, however, was what was on the desk in a room used as an office. "Hey, your Aunt Ivy is wired!"

On the desk was a desktop computer with a large monitor. Andy examined it all: the mouse and commemorative mouse pad, the two CPU towers both connected to the monitor and keyboard, the external drive and several thumb drives in a USB bus, the large speakers, headphones, a telephone, and a small fan. It all looked like the latest equipment. There was even a Kindle Fire sitting next to the mouse pad. The monitor was turned on, showing a screensaver of historic buildings of the world. Behind the monitor sat a colorful cat bed, complete with a large orange cat.

"Hey, Mr. Duck!" Robby reached to pat the cat on the head. The cat responded with a huge yawn and a dramatic paw flourish.

Andy stepped back and examined the top of the desk. Looking at Robby with round eyes, Andy said, "Your aunt knows her way around a computer!"

"She has to," Robby said. "She writes books. Nonfiction about history." He stepped away from a bookcase and held out his hand to direct Andy's eyes to two shelves of similar-sized paperback books in different colors. Andy made a beeline for one of the shelves and reached to touch the spines. He held his head sideways so he could read the titles and author. *The French Revolution, Post-Civil War Reconstruction, The Destruction of Pompeii*—lots more. And all by an I. D. Beaumont. "Is that your great-aunt?"

Robby smiled and nodded. "She's been using the Internet to research some of the materials for the books lately. She even gets books on Kindle, if she can, or she gets a hardback scanned and put on her device. This way she says she has the whole library of Alexandria on her Kindle. In fact she named her Kindle 'Clio' after the Greek muse of history."

"She's so full of trivia about history, she reminds me of Spencer Reid on *Criminal Minds*," Andy said.

Robby nodded enthusiastically. "I know! I just love that guy."

"Me too," Andy said with feeling. "But I wish the other agents would stop putting him down all the time."

"I agree. I wince every time because it reminds me of how people react to me when I trot out some random facts. They get better in the later episodes, though." Robby gave Andy an impish grin. "And that's not all. Come into the other room."

They left the office and went through the closed door of a bedroom.

"Oh, Robby, I don't feel right invading Aunt Ivy's bedroom."

Robby gestured toward a low bookcase. "Just look at these."

On all three shelves were paperback books. Andy pulled one out far enough to see the cover. He looked up at Robby with awe on his face. "These are romances!" He looked again. "They're all by an Adonia Bellaventura. Is that your great-aunt's pen name too?"

Robby nodded again, a look of mischief combined with pride on his face. "That's my great-aunt Ivy. She told me once that writing all the dry books in her professional life and working in a high school with priests and nuns and lots of stuffy people made her write these terribly steamy romances. I mean, look at them. The titles!"

Picking up three of the paperbacks at once, Andy peered at each. They had what might be called quite baroque covers. Women swooned with costumes hanging off their shoulders while men in the uniforms of different armies through time held them up, looking either stricken or savage. He read the titles: *The Duke's Deception, The Prioress of Peterborough Abbey, The Lakeland Lamb's Tale.* "She has a penchant for alliteration."

Robby laughed. "And you've been paying attention in English Lit."

Andy went on looking at the books. He had to get on his knees and lean way down to read the bottom shelf. *Fair and Fortunate Isle, The Husband's Harbinger, The*—"Now wait a minute." He picked up two more and showed them to Robby. On their covers two men were almost naked and clearly looking deeply into each other's eyes. "Gay romance?" Andy asked, incredulous.

Robby looked as surprised as his friend. "I haven't seen those before. I guess she's branching out. You can tell from the quality of the paper on the covers, as well as the printing style and all that, that most of these are a couple or three decades old. These last two are from the last couple of years. Let's see who published them."

He looked at the back covers and then into Andy's eyes. "Dreamspinner Press! I hadn't heard of them. But then, I don't read gay romance."

Andy snatched the book out of his hands. "I do!" He looked at the spines, then said, "I haven't seen these before. I read mostly paranormal and science fiction, not historicals, though." He stopped and looked sheepishly into Robby's face. "Only a few. I found them at a library sale where someone threw those in with regular books. I was just curious."

Robby looked at Andy cautiously. "Oh, I see."

Andy laughed nervously. "I'm getting thirsty," he said.

"I could make tea?"

They turned their heads and watched as Mr. Duck came in the bedroom door. He strolled to the opposite side of the bed and jumped up and lay down. He watched them for a moment, then started to lick his shoulder.

With a decisive nod, Andy shoved the two books back on the bottom shelf and turned and went out the bedroom door.

IN THE kitchen he sat at the table while Robby pulled together the makings of a pot of tea. "Black tea all right? Or do you prefer herbal?"

"Anything," Andy said.

Robby thought a change of topic was called for. "So, it's strange. These things go missing right out from under Aunt Ivy's nose, then a few weeks later they turn up again. And all Aunt Ivy can say is how annoyed she is that they're not exactly in the right position when she finds them again."

Looking around at the items displayed in the kitchen, Andy said, "It's like someone comes in the house and borrows things, then eventually brings them back." He thought for a few minutes. "Did you ever read the Borrower series of kids' books? You know, like *The Borrowers*, *The Borrower Afield*, and *The Borrowers Aloft*. I think there was one more. With Pod and Arrietty—and Homily?"

Robby had poured some loose tea leaves into an infusion ball and now hung it on the inner lid of the teapot. "Oh yeah! I think I read one of them. The boy put a ferret in the mouse hole and the little people had to escape, right?"

"Right. That's at the end of the book, *The Borrowers*. The next book is *Borrowers Afield*. They find a little Borrower boy living in the back garden. And in the final book they move into a little village some guy built so kids would come and pay to see it. It even had a little railroad, I think. They made a TV show of the first one. It had the guy from *Green Acres* in it."

Robby poured the boiling water from a kettle into the teapot. "You mean Eddie Albert?" He brought the teapot to the table, then

CHRISTOPHER HAWTHORNE MOSS

reached into the cabinet for a couple mugs. "Do you take anything in your tea?"

"Yeah, sugar," Andy supplied, then went on, "Yeah, Eddie Albert. I don't remember who played the two women. But that's what they did, the Borrowers, I mean. They would take things for a while from the big people in the house and then later on put them back. Or not."

The two sat and blew on their cups of tea, eventually taking sips and lost in thought.

Finally Robby broke the silence. "So, you got a girlfriend or anything?" he asked. It occurred to him that he didn't know very much about his friend.

Andy seemed distracted. "Naw, I'm not sure I'm even a lesbian."

Robby stared at him. Finally Andy looked up and said, "What?"

Clearing his throat, Robby said, "You said 'lesbian.'"

Andy suddenly blanched. "Oh my God. I did?"

"Yeah, I'm afraid so."

With a look like someone with a very sour stomach, Andy shook his head. "Way to out myself, eh?"

Nodding, Robby said, "I kinda guessed, though."

Andy looked surprised, but then his face cleared. "The jerks in the boys' john?"

"Yeah."

It struck Robby that his sister, Claire, had been acting strangely when she gave the two of them a lift to Aunt Ivy's.

"So, what's the correct term these days for, um, guys who were born girls?" Robby asked tentatively.

Shrugging, Andy replied, "Oh, it changes every few weeks. I have heard AFAB, which means *assigned female at birth*, but I don't like that one. It puts too much emphasis on having been female. I figure once you transition, you know, have all the surgeries and hormones, you're male in all ways except your DNA, so I use FTM if I have to explain things—female to male. But why do I need a label at all? Just call me your friend Andy."

There was a sudden noise from the other room. "Did you hear that?"

Robby thought he heard the sound of a key in the lock and the front door opening from the foyer. "My aunt?" he suggested. But then he heard the sound of the front door closing again. He waited for Aunt Ivy's voice calling out but heard nothing more.

"Is that you, Aunt Ivy?" He got no response. After a few seconds, Robby got up and walked to the front hall, but the door was locked. He glanced out at the steps, but there was no one there. He returned to the kitchen with a puzzled frown on his face.

"Maybe the house is haunted," Andy suggested.

"Aunt Ivy said it could be ghosts, but I thought she was joking. I wonder if she's heard strange noises and never mentioned it."

Andy took another sip of tea, not meeting Robby's eyes. He finally said in a low voice, "So now you know I'm transgender."

Robby shrugged. "Yeah. But it doesn't matter to me. I figure you have a really big challenge. I wanted to punch Smartass out for you. But then the coach came in, and I also thought you might want to do the punching. So I dropped it."

Looking up at him with grateful eyes, Andy said, "Hey, that's cool of you. I appreciate it." He took a couple minutes, then asked, "What do you know about someone being trans?"

Thinking about his conversation with Aunt Ivy about the Chevalier d'Éon and Albert Cashier, Robby finally said, "Not much. I know they now think people have an extra flow of hormones when their brains develop. You know, when you're in your mother's womb. It's sometimes different from the hormones when you're conceived. That means you get born with a male body and then get a female brain, or vice versa."

"That's pretty much it. They say that you can't necessarily tell from a brain scan. It has to do with what percentage white and gray matter you have, but even people who are absolutely 100 percent certain they are the other sex, or I mean gender, might not have that. So there's no way to verify it."

Robby shook his head. "Unless you ask the person. They ought to know which they are. Who needs a brain scan?"

Andy leveled a look of complete gratitude on him. "Wow, are you ever enlightened!" he exclaimed.

"I read everything I can get my hands on."

Smiling broadly, Andy said, "It shows." His face got serious. "That's why I changed schools. Everyone in Olympia knew me as a girl. My parents and I figured it would be easier to try to pass at a new school. But it's not really working out that way."

Robby said, "I dunno. I think you are doing great." He changed the subject. "More tea?" he offered.

"I should go. I have homework."

Andy got up, took his mug, and rinsed it out in the sink and put it on the drainboard. "How are you going to get home?" Robby asked.

"I can walk. I only live about ten blocks from here."

"Let me walk with you," Robby said, standing to take care of his mug and spoon. Andy put a hand on his arm.

"No, I think I need to spend some time alone thinking about how I don't really pass. I'll see you in the morning, okay?"

Robby stood with the mug and spoon in his hand and slowly nodded. "Okay."

Andy smiled shyly and got up on his toes to plant a quick kiss on Robby's cheek. "You better not breathe a word about that," he said in a mock stern voice.

Putting his arms up, Robby said, "Your secret is safe with me."

Andy looked at him and said, "Yeah, thanks."

Robby watched his friend walk to the hallway and out the foyer door. He knew it was all right. He truly didn't care what gender Andy was. Now, if he could just figure out what he was.

CHAPTER 5

ROBBY WATCHED Andy head down the street, then turned to go back to the kitchen. He washed out the tea things and noticed a note on the refrigerator he had missed before.

"I am at the library book sale until 5," it said. That was right; he'd forgotten the book sale was today. Nice of his great-aunt to leave a note, probably for whoever might be expected to stop in. He glanced at the clock. It was just after four thirty, so he might as well wait for her to come home.

He opened the freezer and selected a couple of the neat little Banquet pot pies stacked in every available inch of space. He chose a chicken pie for himself and a turkey one for her. He figured if Aunt Ivy wanted the chicken pie, he would just take the other. He set the oven to the temperature on the box. It had microwave instructions too, but neither he nor Ivy cared for how that left the crust a bit soggy. He turned the timer on the stove to the required amount of cooking time, then set the table and brought out a pitcher of cold water from the refrigerator. It occurred to him that he could have asked Andy to stay for dinner, but he really did seem to want to be alone.

Robby worried a little about how Andy had reacted to his calling attention to his slip. Should he have pretended he didn't

39

hear what he said? No, that could backfire. Andy might know very well what he had let drop and not trust Robby if he pretended he hadn't heard.

The slip made Robby think about his own situation. Puzzling for years whether he was straight or gay, he was now nearly eighteen, and no one seemed to cause his junk to react. There was never any particular object for his excitement. That struck Robby as terribly strange. Shouldn't he at least find *someone* attractive? If he was just not sexual, he figured he would never get an erection, but as he knew from ample experience, he did.

Robby heard a noise at the front door. He went into the hallway and looked down it to see his great-aunt coming in, struggling with four or five brown paper shopping bags.

"Oh, Aunt Ivy, hang on! I'll help. Honestly I don't know why you don't get yourself a cart or at least some plastic shopping bags for when you go to the book sale."

She looked up at him from the bag that had just torn and spilled its contents onto the foyer floor. "Oh, Robby, how nice to see you here. Yes, you're right. I should get some better bags, but I know I'd just forget them at home. Then I would have them and the ripped paper bags both."

Robby took a couple of the bags into the kitchen and set them on the table. Then he went back and gathered the books that had fallen when the bag ripped, and he carried them in and stacked them next to the full bags.

"Robby, how did you get to be such a sweet boy? Your father was never as kind as you are, and your mother—well, she's your mother, and I shouldn't say anything." Aunt Ivy gave him a peck on the cheek, which she had to accomplish standing on her toes.

Robby smiled, beginning to look through the pile of books he had stacked. "It's my pleasure, Auntie. I would have gone with you, but it was during school."

She patted his hand. "I know, dear. And it wasn't really the sale today. It was just the Friends of the Library setting things up for tonight and this weekend."

Looking at her with a wry grin, Robby said, "I see. The book sale hasn't even started yet, and you already have several grocery bags full."

She had taken off her coat and draped it over a kitchen chair, and now she turned to him with her hands on her hips. "Well, you can't expect me to see all these great books and not buy them, can you?"

This time he stooped to kiss her cheek. "No, of course not. These look interesting."

He sat in the nearest chair and picked up one book after another. She had quite a variety. There was a cookbook, an astronomical dictionary, a book on Etruscan art, one on the politics of the James Buchanan era, one on fashion design that looked to be from the 1960s, and several fat books of the almanac sort. He picked out one particular book and started to leaf through it. "This looks good," he observed.

She came back into the kitchen at that moment after taking her coat to the foyer closet. "Oh yes, I got that one for you."

It was a math puzzle book, right up his alley. "Thanks, Aunt Ivy."

She went toward the refrigerator. He was so engrossed in the book he didn't see her take two pot pies out of the freezer and remove the packaging. She leaned over and opened the oven door. "Oh. But there are already two in here! How strange!"

He looked up at that point and laughed. "I put those in the oven. I thought we could have them a little later, when you got home. They still have a while to bake."

"I do love you," she said as she came up behind him, put her arms around his shoulders, and gave them a quick hug. "I see two mugs on the drainboard. Those weren't both yours, were they?"

He glanced over and shook his head. He closed the math book and set it aside. "No, I brought my friend Andy over, and we had tea."

Ivy looked at him expectantly. "Is Andy in the little boy's room or something?" She glanced back at the hallway door.

"No, he left. He said he had to be alone." He realized after he said it that the statement necessarily called for a follow-up question. He blushed.

Ivy beat him to it. "Alone? What happened that he had to spend time by himself?"

Robby just waved his hand in dismissal. "Doesn't matter. I took him upstairs to show him your office and bedroom."

She looked sideways at him. "Is that wise? Might he start taking things?"

Sitting back in his chair, Robby replied, "He knows all about your mysteries. He came over to start helping us unravel it all. That's why I gave him the grand tour."

"Oh," she said. "But you know the captain and the cards are back, right? Back in the house, that is, but not exactly in the right place." She started to get silverware and a couple of glasses for water but then saw he had gotten them already. "Well, aren't you sweet? Way ahead of me."

"Is there anything new missing?" Robby asked.

Ivy checked the timer on the stove and then came over and pulled out a chair and sat down. "Yes. This time it's something quite sentimental. Just a letter. It was written by one of Queen Victoria's nephews to her, not too long before he caught some influenza and died, poor lamb. It's very poignant. I kept thinking, what if that had happened to me? What if you or your sister or a cousin had written it? It made a tear come to my eye. I just don't understand where these things are going and coming back from. I keep thinking a chipmunk gets into the house and steals things, but chipmunks don't return things, do they?" she stated with assurance.

42

She suddenly changed the subject. "So what is your little friend Andrew like?"

Robby couldn't help but smile at her use of the term "little." "Andy is rather short but not what you'd call little. He's pretty squarely built. He has short hair, no facial hair, and he dresses kinda like I do, jeans or regular pants and plaid shirts. He wears boots."

Ivy gave her nephew an indulgent look. "You know I didn't mean what does he look like. Though I am relieved to hear he has no facial hair at his age. What is he like to spend time with?"

Robby was thinking how to describe Andy's personality, especially in light of what he now knew about him, but before he could decide what to say, they heard a knock at the outside kitchen door. He looked at Ivy and said, "Now who's that?"

She jumped up and replied, "Oh, I forgot. It's your Uncle Roger. I asked him to come to dinner tonight." She went to the door and opened it, greeting an average-height, slightly pudgy man in his late fifties. Robby saw his uncle was dressed in his usual suit, nothing fancy, and still sported a moustache. "Hello, Uncle Roger," he called. He had always liked his uncle.

"Hello, Robby." Roger seemed surprised to see him there. "Aunt Ivy." He bent to kiss her cheek.

"I almost forgot you were coming. I'll have to put another pot pie in the oven!" Aunt Ivy bustled over to the refrigerator.

"No, wait, Aunt Ivy. I need to get home. Uncle Roger can have my pot pie."

Aunt Ivy looked balefully between her nephew and her great-nephew. "Oh no, can't you stay?"

A smiling Roger had to shoo Mr. Duck off the chair where he was about to sit. Robby was already getting up. He made a little self-conscious bow to the adults and said, "I can't believe how much homework I have. I better get going. Nice to see you, Uncle Roger."

He headed down the hallway to the front door and retrieved his jacket and hat. The other two followed him out the kitchen door. His aunt was wringing her hands, but Uncle Roger looked vaguely relieved. That puzzled Robby. He always thought his uncle liked him.

He managed to get away and went out onto the step, shutting the front door behind him.

ANDY WALKED along with his hands in his pockets, feeling disgusted for having outed himself as transgender. It bugged him that he still thought in female pronouns. In his dreams he was still a girl much of the time. He knew his counselor said he would get used to thinking of himself as a boy. He was, after all, exactly that. His body might be female, but his brain and, he hastened to add, heart was male.

He had known this since he was eight or nine. He loved stories about men, about spies and soldiers and astronauts and the like. He always insisted on being Brother when he and his friends played house. He didn't have any interest in playing Mother or fussing over the baby dolls.

The girls would look at him when he said he would rather play Brother. "What does Brother do?" they would ask.

He would shake his head and reply, "Mow the lawn?" That seemed to satisfy the girls. But then he realized he was always being sent out of the playhouse or wherever to "go mow the lawn." It was boring, but not as boring as playing house.

As he walked he thought about his plans. He'd had a hysterectomy to put off the inevitable onset of puberty. His mother had thrown a fit until the resistant doctor agreed. He was on testosterone, thus the hunt for chin hairs. He planned to have a mastectomy during the summer before college, eliminating the need to wear a binder. He would probably have bottom surgery someday. He thought about the two types of bottom surgery, metoidioplasty and phalloplasty. With the first they just kinda made the clitoris stick out more and closed up the vaginal opening.

With phalloplasty they actually created a penis, a usually quite functional penis out of the lining of the vagina. It sounded really scary. It took hours and hours and cost a great deal. It was possible it wouldn't work perfectly. But he loved the idea of marching up to a urinal and whipping it out and peeing. Now that would be sweet.

He was almost home when he heard a car slow and pull up on the street near him.

"Hey, freak! Where you goin'?"

He looked up and saw just what he feared. It was Smartass, his two friends, and a couple of girls in an old car. He groaned inside. Then he recognized one of the girls. It was Robby's sister, Claire. Oh, Robby was not going to like to hear about this.

But Andy had to get through the next few minutes first. He looked at Claire as the boys hooted and made rude comments. She didn't look happy. In the car on the way to Robby's aunt Ivy's house, Claire, who had been driving, had been unctuously sweet and kind to Andy. Too sweet and kind. He wondered if Claire knew about him and was just embarrassed. She sure looked embarrassed now. And Andy guessed how Claire had come to have that prized bit of information about his own gender identity. She had gotten it from Smartass and his cronies.

Those charming personages were continuing to drive slowly alongside Andy, calling through the car window. "How come you don't wear a dress? Where's your purse?"

Andy closed his eyes for a moment, hoping the idiots would be gone by the time he opened them again. That almost happened. Just when he opened his eyes, he saw a car coming the other way—a police car. It was just going from Point A to Point B, but the boys apparently decided discretion was the better part of valor. They shut their windows, sped up the car, and left.

Andy's heart was racing, wondering what, if anything, would have happened if the jerks hadn't decided to drive away. He thought about all the things he'd heard happened to transmen. It was basically the same as gay bashing. He thought about the movie

Boys Don't Cry and what had happened to Brandon Teena, being beaten to death. He didn't know if Smartass would go that far. He didn't want to tell his parents or the school officials until he got an idea whether the boys would take things further than what might just be called good-natured ribbing.

He was walking along, looking down at the sidewalk, when he heard a familiar voice. "Andy, hold up a minute!" He spun and saw Robby coming toward him.

"Oh crap, am I glad it's you," he said with a deep sigh.

Stopping where he was and staring at Andy, Robby said, "Why? What happened?"

Andy was horrified to feel tears coming to his eyes. Robby saw and came forward, putting a hand on Andy's shoulder. "Hey, hold on a minute. Was it what I said back at my aunt Ivy's house?"

Miserably Andy shook his head. He managed to get himself under control. "No, it was Smartass. He and his buddies just drove by in a car." Andy looked up into Robby's face. "And Claire was with them."

"Claire? My sister?" he asked. "What is she doing hanging out with them?" He looked at Andy for a moment, his face growing grim. "C'mon, let's go get something to eat. I think we need to talk about this."

As the two of them walked toward the street with all the fast-food joints, Robby said, "Claire is going to be in such deep shit."

CHAPTER 6

THE NEXT morning Robby found Claire sitting at the kitchen table with a stack of cookbooks and a ruled pad and pen in front of her.

"Good morning, Claire. What are you up to?" he asked.

She glanced up at him with a sheepish look on her face. "Um, I'm planning something to take to Aunt Ivy's for Thanksgiving dinner."

He leveled a skeptical gaze on her as he went to pour himself a cup of coffee. "Why?"

She looked back sardonically. "Because it's Thanksgiving?" Her voice was small and tight.

He got himself some canned milk and sugar and brought the coffee to the table. "But Mom always just picks up a pumpkin pie from the supermarket. That's all anyone will expect from us." He sipped his coffee.

A flash of irritation crossed Claire's face. "Well, we don't have to do the same thing every time, you know. I thought I'd make some sort of pumpkin soufflé. Here's a recipe with a chocolate sauce."

He leveled a sardonic look at her. "Give it a rest, Claire. I know where you were last night."

She started to protest but subsided. "That's none of your business."

Robby shrugged. "I suppose it isn't, except that my friend was the person you all taunted."

She dropped her gaze, guilt clearly crossing her face. "I didn't do anything."

He replied succinctly, "Exactly."

Claire looked up with fury in her face. "How do you know what I did? Were you there? I could have really reamed Smartass out for taunting your little trannie friend."

Robby set down his mug and sat back in his chair. "That's not fair. You don't know what Andy is. And you wouldn't risk pissing off anyone if you did."

Their mother walked into the kitchen and went to the coffeemaker. "Good morning, kids. Thanks for making coffee."

"Claire made it," Robby said. "Good morning, Mom."

Sitting down at the table with her mug of black coffee, their mother looked from Robby to Claire. "What's going on here?" she asked, seeing the tension on both their faces. "What's with the cookbooks?"

Robby's lips remained shut.

Claire nervously replied, "I want to make a pumpkin soufflé to take to Aunt Ivy's on Thanksgiving."

Their mother shook her head. "No need. I already ordered a couple of pies from the supermarket."

Robby mouthed "I told you so," earning a sour look from his sister.

"Is Dad going to make an appearance this year?" Claire asked her mother.

Robby faked a spit-take with his coffee, receiving an astounded look from his mother. "Robby, manners!" She turned to Claire. "No, I don't think so. He's going to his girlfriend's family's house, I think. Or maybe they'll go on a weekend trip or something."

Claire glared at Robby. "Hey, Mom, did you know that Robby's been hanging out with some transgender girl named Andy lately? I guess he must be gay or something."

Their mother gave first Claire and then Robby a perplexed look. "Gay? Trans—what's this all about, Robby?"

Refusing to reply, Robby stood and took his partially drained mug to the sink. "I promised Aunt Ivy I would go to her place and rake leaves."

"He's spending lots of time with her. He even took her over to Aunt Ivy's house," Claire stated smugly.

"That's 'him,' not 'her,' and it's none of your business, Claire, who I hang out with. Maybe Mom would like to know the company you keep?" Robby looked at his sister in triumph, then instantly regretted his impulsive words.

Their mother put her own mug down, crossed her arms over her chest, and glared at them both. "Okay, what's all this hostility? And what about this trans girl, and who are you hanging out with, Claire?"

"See you later," Robby said before going into the hall and getting his jacket and hat from the closet. He heard his mother call "Robby, you come back here!" as he went out the front door.

It was no short hike to his Aunt Ivy's house, but he needed the exertion to calm his nerves. He was angry with his sister for getting mixed up with those deadbeats, Smartass and his buddies. He was annoyed with his mother for letting Claire get away with something she didn't even know about yet. He was furious with the boys for tormenting Andy. And he was conflicted about his own feelings about Andy being transgender. It was just too much to handle at once, with the holidays coming up and all. And that reminded him, he was pretty pissed off with his dad for complicating things by having a whole new family that didn't include him.

When he arrived at his aunt's house, he found the front door unlocked and went in. He was surprised to find disorder in the parlor. One of the bookcases was open and the books clearly rearranged. One of the cabinets was likewise open and things removed and set on the floor, on tables, even on one of the chairs. He realized he could hear rummaging going on upstairs and could hear his aunt feverishly muttering to herself. He hung up his coat and hat and took the stairs two at a time.

He found her in her office, searching the drawers in her desk. Her hair was untidy and her face full of distress. "Aunt Ivy!" he exclaimed. "What's wrong?"

She looked up from where she knelt by one of the larger drawers in the desk. "Oh, Robby! I'm so glad you are here. The little commemorative plates! They're gone!" With difficulty she pulled herself to a standing position and ran her fingers through her hair, disordering it further. "I just don't understand what could have become of them! I swear, I'm starting to think I'm losing my mind."

Robby wanted to ask his aunt what plates and where they were missing from, but her agitation drew him to her. He put his arms around her and pressed her face to his shoulder. She let herself lean into him and started to weep, her voice coming out in high-pitched but quiet wails.

"There, there. It will be all right, I promise you. We'll get to the bottom of this."

He guided her to an easy chair to one side of the desk and lowered her into it. He knelt at her feet, his hands on her arms, stroking them, and made comforting noises until her cries quieted.

"Oh, Robby, I'm so terribly afraid. What's happening to me?" She took a handkerchief from the front of her sweater and dabbed at her cheeks.

"There has to be a logical explanation," he comforted her.

Her eyes flashed as she looked into his. "Yes, that I'm losing my mind!"

He flinched at the anger in her voice and eyes. "You are not losing your mind. I saw the empty places where the things that went missing had been. I saw when they were returned. I know you aren't imagining any of this."

Looking desperately at him, Ivy said, "But your uncle Roger says—"

50

"I don't care what he says. I know you. You are neither nuts nor emotional." He made an exasperated noise and stood. "Let's go downstairs and have some tea. We can work this out between us."

He led her down the stairs and into a kitchen chair, then bustled about getting a pot of tea for them both. She sat obediently, patiently waiting for him to finish.

When he was about to set the teapot on the table, she said to him, "I think I need to go to the emergency room."

He opened his mouth to protest but thought better of it. "Maybe you're right. Maybe we should just get you checked and rule out one of the possibilities."

After putting the teapot back on the counter, he went to draw out her chair. She stood and fussed with her hair. "Don't worry about that. I have a comb. And I promise you won't get cooties from it."

She looked at him and suddenly laughed. "Oh, Robby, you are such a card."

When they got to Evergreen Hospital, the orderly took Ivy in a wheelchair back to an exam room in the huge emergency unit. Robby stayed with the nurse who manned the reception desk and answered her questions as best he could. He explained that his aunt had insurance from her employment at the school, now in retirement phase, and that she was worried she was losing her memory. He tried to explain more about the missing items and how he didn't believe there was anything wrong with his aunt, but the nurse just kept giving him irritated and sometimes indulgent looks. She finally stood, put a hand on his shoulder, and told him, "We'll check your aunt out and see what's happening."

He looked up and nodded. "All right. May I go back and see her?"

"Is there anyone in her family—an adult, I mean—who can come to the hospital?" the nurse asked.

He hesitated. "My mother—her niece—I think. Or my uncle Roger. My aunt Norma lives too far away."

51

The nurse pushed a pad toward him and asked him to write his mother's and uncle's names and phone numbers on it. He diligently wrote what she asked while she left the room to check on his aunt.

He didn't know how long he waited. The nurse came back and guided him to a waiting room with coffee and a vending machine. She told him his aunt was with a doctor now and would probably be taken for tests. She said she would call his mother and uncle and they would join him. He sat, fidgeting and tapping his foot, finally starting to calm down. He got up and walked around the waiting room, picked up and discarded magazines, went to peer into the vending machine, got himself a mocha from the automatic espresso machine, and sat down to start tapping his foot again.

"Robby, where is she?" His mother was in Saturday clothes. He realized he had given the nurse her work number, but clearly they had figured it out. "She's back in the emergency room, and I think they're doing some tests."

His mother sat down next to him. "Is Roger here?"

"I don't think so. I told the nurse Aunt Ivy has insurance. She must have thought she was having an aneurism or something."

His mother stood up again. "I'll ask the nurse if we can see her."

Coming back a little while later, Robby's mother told him, "She's having a CT scan. They'll come get us when she's back in her room."

While they were waiting, Uncle Roger arrived. He fussed about and seemed distracted by his aunt's conviction she might be having a stroke. "Why does she think that?" he asked. When Robby explained about the missing items, his face went darker. He shook his head. "But that's not important, where the items are. Do they stay missing?"

Thinking his uncle's reaction was a bit odd, Robby nevertheless reassured him that so far the items were being returned to their homes.

A doctor came in a short time later and explained to his mother and uncle that Mrs. Beaumont was going to be admitted to the hospital for at least one night to monitor her brain health. He explained the CT scans were clear, but he felt she needed to be watched.

"How is she taking it? Being admitted to the hospital, I mean?"

The doctor looked at Robby and answered his question. "She is impatient, of course, and annoyed. Maybe if you could go see her in her new room in the observation unit and find out if she needs anything from home or anyone called…."

Robby was ready to go see her immediately but had to wait until he got the go-ahead that Ivy was in her room. His mother told him, "I have a lot of things to do today. Can you and Roger handle it?"

Robby was annoyed that his mother would bail at a time like this. He reluctantly agreed. She gathered up her purse and coat and took off out the door of the waiting room.

Turning to his uncle, he asked, "I suppose you have things to do too?"

Uncle Roger looked harried. "Yes, but I'll go see her when she's in her room." He seemed irritated and didn't speak to Robby again.

Robby and Roger made their way to the fifth floor of the hospital wing. Aunt Ivy was in a bed in a single room across from the nurses' station. He found her fuming. "The CT scan was clear. I don't know why they have to keep me here. I'm sorry I suggested we come."

Uncle Roger was fawning and condescending. "Now, Ivy, you know they just want to keep you overnight to make sure you're fine."

"But what about Mr. Duck? He's all alone. Who will feed him?"

Robby hurried to reassure her. "I'll go to your house and look after him. I can straighten up for you while I'm there."

Ivy looked at him gratefully. "Look for those plates too, while you're at it. And can you stay there overnight? Mr. Duck isn't used to being left alone in the dark."

"Now, Ivy," Uncle Roger began.

"I'll sleep on the couch," Robby interrupted. "It's no trouble at all." He thought about his fight with Claire and the tension with their mother and was just as happy to be out of their house.

"You're such a good boy, Robby."

His uncle Roger stayed only a short time after, making a big deal of whether Ivy had all she needed and vexing the nurses. When a respiratory technician came in to test Ivy's blood oxygen, Roger asked him if she needed a respirator. The young Asian man reassured him that she was breathing fine on her own, and when Roger querulously demanded to know what would happen if that changed, the man told him he would be in regularly to check and that the nurses would tell him if he needed to come back right away.

"Well, can I give you a lift to Ivy's house or anywhere?" Roger asked Robby when the technician left.

Robby looked at Ivy, who told him, "Yes, it's a long way back there, and I don't want you to have to find a ride later. You go on home. You can call me and check in if you need to."

Reluctantly he accepted his uncle's offer. After reassuring himself and Ivy that everyone, including Mr. Duck, would have everything they needed, Robby followed his uncle to the parking garage to get into Roger's SUV. Roger quickly moved a box from the passenger seat, putting it as far back in the SUV as he could.

As they drove toward Ivy's house, Roger quizzed him about what had been going on with Ivy. He seemed surprised and chewed on his lower lip as he listened.

At Ivy's house Robby let himself in with his key, glad to discover both the front and back doors were locked from their rush to head to the hospital. He found Mr. Duck in Ivy's bedroom on the coverlet on her bed. He sat and stroked the big orange cat on his throat and scratched his ears. "You aren't the one taking all these things, are you?" he asked. The cat gave him an offended look, got up, and jumped off the bed, running out the bedroom door to hiding spots unknown.

CHAPTER 7

THE WHOLE family gathered at Aunt Ivy's house for Thanksgiving. She had come back from the hospital on the previous Monday, and it was driving her crazy how solicitous everybody was toward her welfare. She kept insisting that the CT scans and other tests came back well within healthy ranges. No one had anything to worry about. She was sure she would be around for another twenty years.

One precocious great-grandnephew piped up, "But Aunt Ivy, you would be over a hundred then!"

Present were Aunt Ivy, of course, and Robby, his sister, and mother. Uncle Roger was there, though he had divorced his wife some time before, and she and her kids, a couple of them his too, were back east. Aunt Norma had driven from Portland, Oregon, with her husband, Stephen, and their five kids: the precocious nephew, Micah; the twins, May and Marie; their sister, Toni; and the littlest boy, Craig. One of Aunt Ivy's former fellow teachers from the high school, Sister Mary Elizabeth O'Keefe, was a yearly fixture, and a bag boy from the supermarket, a developmentally delayed adult named Otis, was at dinner for the seventh time.

Micah announced at one point, "That's fourteen people! So you think we have enough pumpkin pie?" which won him a round of laughter, except for Otis, who worried and offered to go to the supermarket for another.

The meal was potluck but orchestrated. The turkey, all twenty-five pounds of it, came out of Ivy's oven golden brown and steaming. Sister Mary Elizabeth made the stuffing, though apparently she and Ivy had a tiff about whether to use Rachel Ray's recipe, which had the stuffing cooked outside the bird and only vegetables inside. Ivy said this was nonsense, that the stuffing lent its aroma to the bird and the bird to the stuffing. "That woman needs to stick to her Italian rock musician and leave us poor folks to our own traditions."

There were mashed potatoes and gravy, green bean casserole, yams with tiny marshmallows, cranberry sauce, rolls supplied by Otis, wine supplied by Aunt Norma and her family, and the pies Robby and Claire's mother had bought. There were "relishes": sweet pickles, black olives, and someone actually found sliced cinnamon apples.

Sister Mary Elizabeth supplied a short standard Catholic grace, which Uncle Stephen finished with "Rub a dub dub, thanks for the grub, yay God" as he did every year.

There was a children's table—a card table set up to the side of the dining room table—where only Norma's and Stephen's kids had to sit. Thankfully Robby and Claire were allowed to sit with the adults, and as a result, they were offered wine. Robby declined, and he soon wished Claire had done the same.

Sometime during the second helpings, Claire started to giggle. She finally blurted out, "Robby's got a girlfriend!"

He looked up at her, startled. "I do?"

Claire giggled some more, then said in a stage whisper, "Her name is Andrea, but she goes by Andy."

His face grew red with irritation. He glanced around the table to see all the adults looking at him with eyebrows raised and questions in their eyes.

All except for Aunt Ivy. She spoke up. "Silly girl. Andy's not a girl. He's a boy!" She looked at the others, smiling. "I met him. Robby brought him over when he brought the pies. Very nice boy. Claire, are you mixing up some other girl's name?"

Claire inserted into the confusion, "But Andy *is* a girl. She just pretends she's a boy."

Aunt Norma said, "Now why would she do that, Claire?"

Uncle Stephen joked, "Maybe she wants to be one."

Robby stared daggers at Claire, but then he glanced at his mother, who sat looking confused.

"I thought Andy was the new boy in town? Isn't he?" their mother asked.

"She's a trannie," shared Claire. "She had an operation to remove her uterus and breasts." Claire stumbled over the *S*'s in "uterus" and "breasts."

Robby had a mouthful of stuffing and gravy, so he wasn't easy to understand when he protested Claire's sharing Andy's private business. He shook his head but didn't correct her about the timing of Andy's top surgery.

Micah had gotten up from the children's table and stood by his father. "Why would she do that, Dad?" He looked at his mother. "What's a trannie?"

Robby stood up at that point, throwing his napkin onto his plate. "Claire, that's enough!" he snapped.

Their mother looked from son to daughter and back. "Claire, are you saying that Andy is having a sex change?"

Stephen got up and grabbed Micah's arm to lead him out of the dining room.

Aunt Ivy cleared her throat and sat with her fists clenched. She said in a clear, hard voice, "Be quiet, everyone. This is our family Thanksgiving dinner, and we are going to eat it with peace and understanding, just as the Sister's prayer said. Andy is his own person, and what he does is his business. 'Judge not that ye be not judged' is what scripture says."

Claire looked at Ivy, all innocence. "I didn't condemn her. I just said she was a trannie."

Robby left the table and went to the hall closet, where he retrieved his jacket and hat.

Ivy caught up with him as he was shutting the front door behind him. She reached out and grasped his coat sleeve. "Robby, please. Don't let Claire ruin your Thanksgiving. Come back and finish your dinner."

He looked at her, his eyes still flaming. "Ask her who she's been spending time with and what she's been doing. Claire is not the angel you think she is. She has some bad friends."

Ivy loosed her grip on his jacket, and he fled down the stairs and to the sidewalk.

Robby walked fast, heading nowhere in particular. He kept imagining the conversation back at Ivy's after he left. Uncle Stephen would be chastening Micah for simply asking the questions, and Aunt Norma would be telling him it was just innocent curiosity. Claire would be playing all innocent with big, shocked eyes. Their mother would be asking for details. Otis would just keep eating, and Sister Mary Elizabeth would be dumb with confused horror. Aunt Ivy would eat on in stern silence. The youngest children would sit with big round scared eyes, and the twins would have their heads together whispering. But at least he didn't have to listen to it.

He started to wonder where he was going. He seemed to be more or less headed to his family's apartment, but then he realized he was in front of Andy's condo. Andy had pointed it out to Robby once when Claire dropped him off at home. He stood looking at the flats of condos all in a row. The shorter building down the row was either a resident clubhouse or pool or some other thing. He remembered which of the condos Andy had gone into and set his steps in that direction, then rang the bell when he reached the door.

A tall, bearded man answered when he reached to knock. "May I help you?" he asked. He had short hair, a black turtleneck, and a bright red vest on over it. He wore glasses and was holding a dinner napkin in his hand.

"I'm sorry to disturb your dinner. I'm Andy's friend Robby. Is he here?"

Andy appeared at his father's elbow. "Well, of course I am. It's Thanksgiving, after all. Why aren't you at your Aunt Ivy's?"

The man stepped back and gestured for Robby to come in, which he did, nodding at Andy. "Hi, Andy. They… um… got done with their dinner, and I thought I'd come see how you were doing."

A large woman with dark hair and wearing a sweater and stretch pants came toward him, smiling.

Andy hastily introduced them. "Robby, this is my mom. Mom, this is Robby, my friend from school. And this is my dad. And my brother, Gabe."

Mrs. Kahn beamed. "Robby, how good it is to meet you. Andy has told us all about you. Come in. Gabe, please go get another chair and another place setting. You will sit with us while we finish our dinner, won't you?"

Gabe was already out of the room, but when he came back in with plates and silverware, Robby saw he was a tall, possibly ten-year-old boy wearing a yarmulke. Robby realized Andy's father was wearing one too, but Andy wasn't. He gave Andy a questioning look, but Andy didn't seem to notice. Then he remembered Andy saying he didn't follow all the observances, and assumed that was why.

Robby found himself seated next to Andy at the table. Robby respectfully declined Mrs. Kahn's offer of food, saying he was already full. He accepted a glass of iced tea when offered but turned down the wine. He sat big-eyed while the family finished eating and just listened as Andy's mother babbled on about how wonderful it was to see her older son had a nice friend here in the city.

Mr. Kahn asked Robby about his family, about school, about where he lived, and smiled and nodded sagely at his answers. Gabe was quiet. He just ate and watched Robby. Andy seemed nonplussed by Robby's appearance.

When they'd finished eating, Mrs. Kahn suggested Andy take Robby up to his room to show him his computer while she got pie and whipped cream for them all.

Once upstairs, Andy looked hard at Robby. "Why did you really come?"

Robby gave him an apologetic look. "Family stuff, an argument. I got mad and walked out."

Andy's eyebrows went up. "Jeez," he said. Then he asked, "Claire?"

Nodding, Robby looked around for somewhere to sit. He finally just sat on the edge of the bed. The room looked like his own, with a desk and computer, neutral-color drapes and bedspread, and nothing but boy's things around, except for a teddy bear on the bed by the pillow.

"Nice room," he said.

Andy put his hands on his hips and tilted his head. "No girl stuff, huh?"

Robby glared. "No, of course not."

Andy sat down on the desk chair at the computer. "So she knows and she spilled the beans."

Robby looked at him earnestly and said, "I didn't say anything to her about you one way or another."

"I believe you. It's that crowd she's hanging with now," Andy said. He looked long at Robby and finally asked, "Don't you have any questions?"

Robby stared at him. "No. Why should I? It's obvious you're a guy, and you dress and act like a guy."

Andy's face softened for a moment. "Thank you" was all he said. He looked at his knees, where he had his hands clasped. "You want to listen to some music or something?"

Shrugging, Robby asked, "What do you have?"

Andy turned to his computer's monitor. "I have the whole world, right here." He moved the mouse, which awoke the monitor, then double-clicked on an icon on the desktop. "I like oldies mostly, like early seventies, but I have stuff from all times. Even the Renaissance."

After getting up to look over Andy's shoulder at the monitor, Robby scanned the list of titles on the screen. "Hey, you have Adam Lambert!"

He highlighted the album titled *Trespassing* and clicked to start it playing. Soon Adam's voice was belting out a line about a sign that said No Trespassing. Both boys joined in on singing the chorus.

They laughed when they looked at each other, pointing their thumbs at their respective chests.

When the song was over, Andy reached over to switch the player off. "Time for pie!" he announced.

Robby followed Andy into the living room, where plates of pie had been set out with forks. Each slice had a mountain of whipped cream on it. Andy and Robby took seats on the couch and each accepted a plate of pie. It was obvious from the first bite that the pie was homemade, and the whipped cream too.

Andy's mom started to explain that the family had moved north so Andy's dad could take a job with Microsoft.

"He knows," Andy interrupted.

Mrs. Kahn looked at Andy. "He knows… about you? How does he know?" She looked challengingly at him.

"I outed myself by accident," Andy interrupted to save Robby explaining.

Mrs. Kahn and her husband exchanged looks. She looked back at Robby. "I suppose that can't be helped. I told Andy he needs to do what makes him feel comfortable. If he wants people to know, that's fine. If not, he needs to be ready to explain away slips."

Robby looked from Mrs. Kahn to her husband and her two sons. "You are so accepting. I wish the world was more like you."

Mr. Kahn echoed, "Me too."

Gabe shrugged. "Me too. I don't care if she's my sister or he's my brother. He's a pain in the butt either way."

His impish smile countered the condemnatory looks from both his parents. Mrs. Kahn said, "Oh, Gabriel!"

Sitting, eating pie, and drinking more iced tea, Robby found himself relaxing. He listened to the Kahns and their kids talk about everything, from school to music to television shows to the news. Gabe chimed in for a while, then excused himself to go listen to "tunes" on his iPod.

Finally Robby couldn't ignore any longer that he was going to have to go home and face the music. He got up, shook hands with Mr. and Mrs. Kahn, and went out the front door after picking up his jacket and hat. Andy followed him.

"That was really nice," Robby said. "Your family is great."

Andy smiled at him. "It was touch and go at first. Even as liberal as they are, it was hard for them to accept when I first told them. But then they joined Parents and Friends of Lesbians and Gays and also talked to that guy Aidan Key from Gender Odyssey. Now you'd think they invented transgenderism."

"Gender Odyssey?" Robby asked.

"It's an organization to help transgender people and their families get information and support," Andy explained. "It's based right here in the Seattle area. The director, Mr. Key, is a transman himself and works with school districts on policies to deal with transgender students. I got to meet him, and he helped me find some support groups for trans kids."

"And Gabe?"

"You heard him. I'm a pain in the butt either way."

As he zipped up his jacket, Robby asked Andy, "What do they think about Smartass and all the stupid things that have happened at school?"

Andy shook his head and put his finger to his lips. "I didn't tell them about any of it. They have a hard enough time thinking of me out there in the cold, cruel world. They don't understand that I can handle it, that I have to handle it. For my whole life. If I told them, they'd be at the school in a flash demanding justice and discipline and equal rights and all that stuff. Nothing serious has happened. People are learning."

Putting a hand on Andy's shoulder, Robby said, "I just hope it stays that way." He squeezed. "Now I have to go home and find out what Mom thinks of what Claire did."

"Take one on the chin for me," Andy said, grimacing. Then he grinned. "Good luck. And happy Thanksgiving."

Back at his family's apartment, Robby found his mother sitting in the living room smoking the first cigarette she'd had in years.

"Where's Claire?" Robby put his jacket and hat away.

"In her room. You and I need to talk." Robby's mother sat, looking stern.

Robby sighed and sat down on a chair across from the couch. "I can't share private things, but what do you want to know?"

The look on his mother's face was strained. "Robby, are you gay?"

Gay? Is that what she thinks? He shook his head. "No, Mom, I'm not gay." To himself he said *I wish I knew.*

CHAPTER 8

IT WAS early December, and Andy sat in the lunchroom with a notebook, pen, and a big sheet of newsprint in front of him.

"What are you doing?" came Robby's voice.

Andy looked up, startled out his concentration. "Planning part of a New Year's Eve party," he said somewhat vaguely.

Taking a seat next to him at the cafeteria table, Robby looked at the large piece of newsprint. "Oh, PFLAG! I didn't know they did parties."

Andy confirmed, "Oh yeah, people in PFLAG want to get together, but there's not always a place conducive to all our differences. I mean, there are gay guys and lesbians, genderqueer, transgender people, their parents and siblings, a minister or two, and a rabbi. That's a pretty mixed group, and when the festivities start up, it's a blast."

Robby considered. "I suppose when it's midnight you'll get a lot of different kinds of people kissing."

Andy gave him an appreciative smile. "Yeah, exactly."

Robby appeared to think for a while, then looked at the people at their table and in the room. "So you're okay with people seeing you work on this in here?"

Rather than being at all offended, Andy nodded. "I figure people know there's something different about me, and this just lets them guess. They probably think I'm a gay guy or a lesbian, anyway. But I could be an ally."

Robby gave him a wry look. "Yeah, right."

Laughing, Andy punched him in the shoulder. "Hey, that's some muscle. You're still working out?"

Robby struck a pose, flexing his bicep with a big shit-eating grin on his face. He said in a Sylvester Stallone voice, "Yeah." He went on, "Yeah, I figure if I get real pumped, there's only a couple of ways it can go, and either way it's all good. I can take out anyone who hassles girls or gay guys or you, or I can get so butch, I'll...." He trailed off, blushing.

Andy gazed at his red face. He decided not to pursue it, since Robby had always respected his privacy, and he wanted to respect Robby's. Instead he said, "Oh, I see, you plan to defend me against the big bad bullies? What makes you think I can't handle them myself? What a dick you are."

Starting to protest, Robby stopped and considered his friend. "You're right."

Andy laughed aloud. "What? That you're a dick?"

Robby said, "I'm thinking about going out for wrestling."

Andy decided to keep his mouth shut about the intimate contact with other boys that Robby would have to endure. "I wish they did coed wrestling."

Looking at him with a sardonic lift to his eyebrows, Robby said, "What do you care? You're in boys' gym class."

Andy's face took on a look of pleased surprise. "Oh yeah, that's right!" He jumped up from the table and mimed a wrestling stance.

Robby couldn't help but laugh uncontrollably.

He gestured to the notebook. "So what's your role in all this?"

Pulling the notebook to him, Andy said, "I'm sort of the youth team planner. I get to decide what the kids and teens are going to do."

Robby nodded slowly. He tilted his head to look at Andy. "Want help?"

Andy's eyebrows went up. "You?"

"Why not me?"

"You aren't gay!" Andy protested.

"How do you know? Besides, I could be an ally. Or a family member. Maybe Claire's a lesbian." He joined Andy in a laugh at the very idea.

"You never know." Andy shrugged. "Okay. You're on. The next support meeting is on the nineteenth, but the party committee is sooner. Can you come over at six thirty on Tuesday? My mom will give us a ride. *Of course* she's on the party committee. She plans all parties all the time. Mazel tov!"

BACK AT Robby's home, tensions were alternately ignored and very much in evidence. Claire kept giving Robby sideways looks. Their mother didn't speak to Claire at all about her recent choice of friends, as far as he could tell. He was angry—Claire could always wrap her mother around her little finger—but he decided to drop it. Maybe nothing would come of it.

THE NEXT Tuesday Robby presented himself at the Kahns' front door. Andy opened it and greeted him with a really broad smile. "I'm so glad you're here." He led Robby into the kitchen, where Mrs. Kahn was packaging a plate of cookies.

"Oh, Robby. Andy said you were coming. Welcome! Someone always brings cookies or brownies. I always do too. Better to err on the side of generosity. We can always bring the extras home."

Andy snatched a cookie and gave it to Robby. "Here ya go."

He took it and said to Andy, "Your mom is so nice."

Mrs. Kahn looked at him oddly. "I'm sure your mom is too."

"Well, she never makes cookies."

Andy took one for himself and started to munch. "Mmm, peanut butter. With chips. I love them." He looked again at Robby. "Does your mom know you're coming with us?"

Shrugging, Robby said, "No. She wasn't home. Neither was Claire. So I just left a note on the fridge."

Mrs. Kahn gave Robby the plate of cookies to carry out to the SUV. He asked, "Doesn't Gabe come to these things?"

"He isn't on the party committee. But he and my dad will be at the party itself."

They arrived at the First United Methodist Church on 108th in plenty of time. There were lots of parking spaces in the lot. They went into the basement of the church and found the minister and a couple of kids setting up tables for the meeting.

A woman came in with a cardboard box full of things for the team to go through.

"Hi, Amy," Andy said. "This is my friend from school, Robby. He wants to help."

She smiled and put a hand on Robby's shoulder. "Cool."

Others started to come in. There were a couple of teens, a parent or three of either gender, a young woman who could have been a man, and just as they were about to sit down to talk, a man arrived with a big white beard just like Santa. When he spoke he had the "accent" that people often ascribed to gay men, so Robby accepted him as gay.

He sat listening to everyone, growing more and more comfortable as the group went around and introduced themselves.

"I'm Reverend Ronald Lucas. I'm straight. I've been a member of PFLAG for about sixteen years."

"And he's the pastor of this church," added a woman sitting next to him. "I'm Pat, Ron's wife, and I've been a member for just as long. Oh, and I'm straight."

Each person gave his or her, or in the case of the man/woman, zer name and orientation and said how long they had been involved with the group. Robby was intrigued by the genderqueer person who asked for the unusual pronoun. He had heard of genderqueer people but didn't think he had ever met one.

He noticed that Andy introduced himself as an "FTM" or "a trans man" and said he and his mother had just joined this particular PFLAG the past summer when they moved to the Eastside from Olympia. Mrs. Kahn introduced herself as Ruth, said she was Andy's mother, and mentioned the peanut butter cookies.

Then it was Robby's turn. He went pale. "Um, I'm Robby. I'm Andy's friend from school, and this is my first meeting."

The genderqueer person, whose name was Phoenix, piped up, "So what are you? Gay or straight or what?"

He looked blank. "I don't know yet," he replied truthfully.

Phoenix said, "Oh. That's a new one."

The minister, Rev. Lucas, inserted, "Not so new. We've all been there at some point."

Robby noticed that Andy was looking at him strangely. He realized they had never talked about his confusion about his own sexuality. He gave him a smile, and Andy nodded, then turned to the group to start the activities.

After, as they waited by the car in the parking lot for Mrs. Kahn to finish talking to two of the other parents, Andy said to Robby, "So was that true? You really don't know? It wasn't just a way to avoid saying you were gay or whatever?"

He gave him a strained look. "It's true. I really don't know. And maybe we can talk about it some other time?"

BESIDES PLANNING the PFLAG party, the two boys were getting ready for Christmas and Hanukkah with their families. Robby didn't know anything about the Jewish holiday, but Andy knew all about Christmas, though his take on it was decidedly commercial.

"I remember going to the department store to sit on Santa's lap and tell him all about the gifts I wanted him to buy for me."

"Buy for you?" Robby asked, acting surprised. "Santa doesn't buy presents. The elves make them."

Andy just shrugged. "I didn't know that. And I thought Santa was some old Jewish teacher from Hebrew school. I didn't go there. I refused. But it was a terrible shock when I found out that Santa Claus was goyim. Explained why he had a Spanish accent that one year, though."

Robby chuckled. "Did your mom and dad take you to see Santa?"

"Oh yeah, every year. How about you?"

"Not very often. We used to go sometimes when Dad still lived with us, but Mom was too busy after the divorce. Claire and her friends went by themselves. I just didn't see the point."

Giving him a sympathetic look, Andy said, "That's kinda sad."

Robby looked back, surprised. "It wasn't sad. I just grew out of it early. Claire was so mercenary about it. She would take a list, typed and organized by priority, and once she was on his lap, she would expound on all the things she wanted and what stores she had seen them at and which ones were better quality, though having brand names seemed to be what made them better quality."

Andy was laughing. "Did she get what she wanted?"

Robby shook his head. "Nope. Mom couldn't afford it and was just too busy anyway. She always got me underwear and socks and one year a matching scarf and mittens."

"Wow...."

The two worked steadily at the party planning, getting together to make favors and practice songs. Mrs. Kahn baked and baked. Gabriel joked about spiking the punch with Manischewitz wine. Mr. Kahn gave him a stern, admonishing look, to which Gabe cried, "I was just kidding!" Then he winked at his older brother.

When it came time for the actual holidays, Robby and Andy decided to split the difference and just do the winter solstice for their own gift giving. Robby had money from chores he did for Aunt Ivy, but she suggested he give Andy something from her own odd collections. He chose a pocket watch she assured him was not worth a great deal. He decided it was a good idea and just promised more chores.

When the two went out to McDonald's for their winter solstice event, Robby opened his gift first. He was delighted to find it was a book about the history of scholastic competitions in the United States.

When Andy opened the ornately wrapped box with the watch in it, he was flabbergasted. "Robby, this is too expensive," he protested.

"Don't ruin it!" Robby said in reply. "Gifts are from the heart, not from the cash register. Besides, all it cost me were some snowy sidewalks shoveled, and who knows how long it will be before it actually snows and sticks here in the Northwest."

The night of the New Year's Eve party, the Methodist Church basement was festive with evergreen bows and a highly ornate Christmas tree, with tables set with a variety of treats and punch. The gay Santa had decorated the tree with all sorts of miscellaneous ornaments, including rainbow flags, discs with funny sayings on them like "Don we now our *gay* apparel", a silhouette of a unicorn, and rainbow and lavender bows.

The group played various games and listened to Christmas carols. Rabbi Cohen led them all in a few rounds of spin the dreidel that almost turned into a kissing game. Robby noticed a couple of girls who kept making goo-goo eyes at each other and whom he saw in the darkened hallway later wrapped in a passionate embrace. He averted his eyes as he headed for the men's room.

At midnight everyone gathered with glasses of punch and did the countdown to twelve o'clock. Andy told Robby that the tradition was whoever you kissed at midnight was the person you would be with the same time next year. They looked into each other's eyes, Robby's a little narrowed, but when twelve was struck and the others were proclaiming "Happy New Year!", he and Andy found themselves with their lips locked together.

Afterward Andy looked at Robby, curious. "Anything?"

Robby shrugged. "Nothing, but it was really, really nice."

Andy smiled.

WHEN ROBBY got home that night, he found himself completely alone. He knew his mother hadn't gone out. He looked for a note but didn't find one anywhere. He debated going to bed or staying up to find out what happened.

At about 2:30 a.m., as Robby was dozing in front of the living room television, he heard the key in the front door lock. He looked up and saw Claire, her head down, scurry across the room and into the hallway. He heard her bedroom door open and shut with a slam. He glanced back at the entryway and saw his mother putting away her coat and hat. She turned toward him, her hands on her hips, and said, "I need a drink."

She headed into the kitchen and got herself a neat Scotch. Robby followed her in and looked nervous as she gulped the drink down. "Mom…," he began. "I didn't know there was any booze in the house." There hadn't been since his mother had come to grips with the fact that she was drinking too much.

His mother shot him a fiery look. "Ask your sister about it, why don't you? She's the one who got arrested." She slammed down the highball glass and said, "I'm going to bed."

Robby stood in the kitchen, stunned. *Arrested? How? What?* He didn't know how he was going to get to the bottom of the situation.

CHAPTER 9

THE NEXT day Claire hung out in her room. She was so grounded it wasn't funny. Robby never spoke to her, and their mother was out all day, so he learned nothing.

He was about to pick up the phone to call Andy when it rang. He answered it to find Max on the other end of the line.

"I was going to text you, but I figured I'd take a chance on your being awake. How was the party at PFLAG last night?" Max asked.

Robby of course had told Max, Luis, and Rhonda about his and Andy's working on the PFLAG party. Rhonda had been vaguely interested, Luis was too focused on some big family do he was going to, but Max had been unusually quiet about New Year's Eve. So Robby was surprised he had been the one to ask the next day.

"It was great. Very relaxed and fun. There were lots of cakes and cookies and punch, and we played various games."

Max made generally approving noises, then went on, "So what kind of people go to something like that?"

Robby was unsure at first what Max meant. Then he remembered that what had started to become normal and everyday to him would seem strange or exotic to someone else. "Oh, well,

Andy, of course. And his mom. There were other younger people, their parents and siblings, and there was one guy who looked just like Santa Claus and was very gay. There were other gay guys and lesbians and someone I think is genderqueer."

"Gender what?" Max asked.

"Genderqueer. That means you don't believe you fit any particular pigeonhole, male or female." Robby marveled at how fluent he was with all these issues he had known little or nothing about at the beginning of the school year.

Max said hesitantly, "Like bisexual?"

Robby shook his head, even though Max couldn't see it over the phone. "No, it's different. You might be bisexual or you might be something else. It's kind of hard to explain. I suppose the best thing I can do is say you're kind of neutral."

"Oh," said Max, though he didn't sound like he understood anything. There was a pause in the conversation. Then he asked, "And this Santa Claus guy? You say he was gay? How old was he?"

Robby thought awhile. "Gee, I don't know. Sixty? He had white hair and a long white beard."

Max said "Oh" again, but this time he sounded surprised. "I guess I hadn't thought a gay man could be old. You'd think your interest in sex would die down by the time you were sixty."

Fighting the urge to laugh aloud, Robby said, "He didn't bring a lover, but I don't know if he has one. He just works with the kids at some center for gay and lesbian and transgender youth. He's a really nice, fun guy. He brought most of the decorations for the tree from the charity store at the center."

"And he didn't hit on you or Andy?"

Now Robby had to laugh. "No, why would he?"

Max took a while to answer. "Oh, I don't know. Don't gay men go for boys?"

The situation was so absurd, and Robby was so full of shock from the events of late last night, that he didn't know what to say. "I don't think so" was all he could think of.

There was another silence. Max finally said, "Well, I suppose I should go. I think my family is finally getting up. I'm starved for breakfast." He went on as if voicing an afterthought. "Why did Andy go? Is he gay or something?"

Stunned into silence, Robby realized belatedly that he hadn't thought about what people who didn't know Andy was transgender would think about his going to PFLAG. He didn't feel right about sharing Andy's gender identity with others without his permission. He knew Andy had wanted to kiss him, but he didn't know if that made Andy gay or what. He hadn't thought about it. If you were female and were into a guy, you would be straight. But Andy was a guy. Did that make him gay? It was enough to make his head spin. And worse, Robby wondered what it made him.

The silence went on too long. Max was getting impatient. But his instincts must have been pretty good, since he didn't press. "Well, whatever. I'm glad you had a good time. Are you going to join the group? Maybe sometime I could go with you? If that's okay, I mean."

Max's offer to come with them startled Robby more than anything else he'd said. He thought about outing Andy. He thought about Max's more bigoted comments. He thought about whether Max was into Andy and was surprised to feel a twinge of jealousy.

"Gee, I don't know. I guess you could come." Robby felt like hanging up on Max. "I gotta go. I gotta call Andy."

"Oh, okay. Bye, then. I'll see you at wrestling tryouts."

"Yeah, see you."

Robby had forgotten all about wrestling and the tryouts. They were right after school resumed. He knew Max was into wrestling. He wondered if Andy would be too.

ANDY RAN into Max, Luis, and Rhonda near the school's front door a couple of days later. "Hey, you guys. How was your holiday?" he asked.

Luis seemed effusive. "My older brother got a car! He's going to let me buy his old one!"

"A car? For Christmas?" Andy was pleased but surprised at the extravagance of the gift.

"It was my papi's old car. It's a Dodge Dart but in really good shape."

"If that old tank is your brother's car, what are you going to get from him?" Max had a mocking tone in his voice and an amused look on his face.

Luis realized Max was going to make fun of him and answered defiantly, "Wouldn't you like to know?"

Robby joined the group. "Wouldn't Max like to know what?"

Luis shrugged. "What kind of car my brother is selling me."

Robby looked at Max. "It's his old VW bus. It needs a lot of work. I told Luis I would help. The chassis is in pretty sweet condition, though. If he fixes up the mechanics, he'd have a real vintage baby."

Rhonda cooed, "Hey, man, groovy. Hippie bus. Marijuana is legal now, so we could get some weed and take a *Magical Mystery Tour*. We could paint Peter Max stuff all over the outside."

They all looked at her. "Just sayin'."

Luis nodded with his eyebrows up and his lips in a considering grimace. "We could do that!" He looked at Rhonda. "Far out!" He put up his hand to high-five, and she reciprocated.

ROBBY FOUND time to talk to Andy alone. "My sister got arrested," he said sardonically.

Andy stared at him, astounded. "She did? What did she do to get busted?"

They continued down the school corridor. "I'm not exactly sure, since no one is talking to me at home, but I think it has something to do with Smartass."

Andy nodded slowly. "Wonder what he got her into."

"I suppose we might hear something at school. Have you seen any of them yet? My sister is at school today, but she's a year behind me, so I don't have any classes with her."

They strolled along, both deep in thought. Then Andy said, "Oh well, Hey, I heard that the schedule for the Quiz Kids' events is coming out this week. We'll find out which other schools we'll be competing with."

Stopping in the hallway where he stood, Robby shook his head. "Oh damn, I forgot all about that. I hope it doesn't interfere with wrestling. I'd hate to have to miss either one."

His mouth open with surprise, Andy protested, "You have to come to Quiz Kids! We can't win without you!"

Robby shrugged. "I guess we'll just have to see which I have to drop, if either."

LATER MAX and Robby stood in line in their gym clothes, waiting for their turns to try out for the wrestling team. "This is your first tryout, isn't it?" Max eyed Robby strangely.

Robby, who had been distracted, nodded. "Yeah. I really buffed up this summer. I was in no shape last year." Noticing Max's appraising stare, he flexed a bicep. "Not too shabby, huh?"

Max gave him a quick up-and-down look. "Fuck, yeah," Max said, but he had trouble getting the words out. He turned sideways and looked down the line behind them. He seemed to adjust his gym shorts. "I don't see Andy."

Robby looked the same way. "No, he's not going in for wrestling. He's afraid it will interfere with the schedule for Quiz Kids."

Max looked at Robby. "Aren't you worried about that too? I mean, aren't you their star player?"

Robby shrugged. "Dunno. I'll cross that bridge when I come to it."

School was starting to get more complicated for him. Here he wanted to participate in both wrestling and Quiz Kids. He was trying to find out what Claire was up to. He was worried about taking too many classes and having too many extracurricular activities. And now Max was acting all squirrelly.

"Hey, dude, you okay?" he asked Max.

Max first looked surprised, then put back his shoulders and gave Robby a defensive but challenging look. "I'm cool, bro. Nothin' to it. I got my eye on the game, you know." He waited a moment and said, "What's your problem?"

"Nothin'," Robby lied.

"Hey, I almost forgot. I found out what went down with your sister Claire on New Year's Eve. Nothing really big."

"Oh yeah? What happened?"

Max leaned toward Robby in a conspiratorial manner. "Smartass and his boys got busted for stealing brews from a convenience store. I guess the girls were in the car. And rumor says Smartass had his uncle's gun. They busted the whole bunch of them."

Robby's face wore a wondering look. "Claire? Busted with beer?"

Max nodded with a look of triumph on his face. "And stolen beer at that, and with a weapon-involved crime. I'm surprised they aren't all kicked out of school."

"Czerwinski!" The wrestling coach's assistant called Robby's name.

"Go for it, bro," Max said.

Afterward the two boys compared notes. "I made it," Max crowed.

"I made second squad," admitted Robby, not as disappointed as he thought he'd be.

"Oh yeah? How come?"

"I just don't know the moves. I'm strong enough, but I don't know dick about wrestling. I thought I did from class, but not well enough to make the team."

Max eyed Robby speculatively. "I could teach you."

Robby grinned broadly. "Hey, yeah. We could do that. Maybe I can join the team if there's an injury or something."

Max grinned but looked uneasy. "That sounds pretty harsh. But hey, *que sera sera.*"

AT HOME that evening, Robby found himself sitting across the dinner table from Claire. To both their amazement, their mother had decided to cook a meal, a stew with carrots and potatoes to be precise, and they were "going to eat dinner like a family, damn it," as she said. Claire and Robby gave each other astounded looks but did their best to act like it was no big deal.

Just before their mother told Claire to clear away the plates, she said to Robby, "Things are going to change around here. I realize I've been too busy and harried, and we need at least a semblance of some sort of stability in this apartment. From now on Claire and I will cook dinner, and we will eat as a family. You two will have a set list of chores, but in the evening you will first do your homework. Once Claire is done with her punishment, she can go out in the evening, but she will have to clear with me first who she goes out with and where they go and what they do. So long as you mind your p's and q's, young man, you can do as you please. Is that understood?"

Claire had come back to the table and exchanged a look with her brother.

"Yes, ma'am," Claire said at the same time as Robby.

"How long do you think this will last?" Robby asked Claire when they ran into each other in the hallway before bed.

She just shrugged. "It's not as bad as all that. The guys just shoplifted some beer. We didn't even go into the convenience store with them. I don't know why the girls got busted."

Robby peered at her. "But I heard Smartass had a gun!"

Claire rolled her eyes at him. "Oh God, the rumor mill is going great…. Umm, guns… is it? No, he didn't have a gun. Why would he use a gun to steal a couple of six-packs?"

Robby nodded. "Good point."

Robby texted Andy when he was in bed.

It's a mess here. Claire really fucked up. I've got to finish my homework.

Okay. You okay with that?

He sighed. *Whatever.* He just didn't know.

CHAPTER 10

"HEY, CHECK this out, bro," Andy called to Robby as he joined him for lunch. He had the schedule for Quiz Kids in his hands. Andy excitedly read, "We're competing with teams from Bellevue, Tacoma, and Redmond." As he approached Robby, he read the last line on the schedule. "Oh no. The finals are in Olympia."

"What's wrong with Olympia?" Robby asked.

Andy felt sick. "People knew me as a girl there."

Robby stared at him a moment, then said, "Oh. And you think there might be people competing or in the audience from your school?"

Andy was sure his expression said that that was exactly what he was thinking.

"I guess we should wait to see if we even make the finals before we worry about stuff like that," Robby suggested.

"Since I didn't make the main wrestling squad, at least I won't have any conflict with the Quiz Kids schedule, unless a wrestler from the first squad is injured and Coach asks me to compete."

"Good thing, since you're our star player," Andy said.

Robby glanced at the schedule. "The first event is next Monday at East Sammamich. We'll have to practice this weekend to get ready for it."

Andy nodded, then asked, "What do you think of Pollack's biology class topic this semester?"

Robby seemed startled at the change of subject. "You don't think we'll get questions about that, do you?"

"Of course not. Or at least, I would be amazed. Sexuality is hardly what they usually ask about, is it?"

"No. I just wondered why you brought it up," Robby said. "I dunno, I guess it's an improvement over no sex education at all."

When Mrs. Pollack's class finished its semester on genetics, they moved on to human sexuality. There were the usual giggles and rude remarks, but Mrs. Pollack's grim looks put the damper on those. While they would cover reproduction, Mrs. Pollack said, the plan was to cover sexuality more generally. Everyone was mystified by what that could mean. Andy looked forward to finding out but also feared just how embarrassing it would turn out to be.

He also wondered, given how good the school administration had been in dealing with his trans status, if they would cover GLBT issues.

MAX STARTED Robby on wrestling practice Saturday morning. They had to use the playground at Robby's apartment complex since the school was closed and there was nowhere they could use in Max's neighborhood. The surface was surprisingly crumb rubber, allowing for softer falls. It was the Seattle area and therefore not a real chilly winter, but nevertheless the two boys were in sweat clothes and knit caps.

Max started them out by pointing out where a person's strengths and weaknesses were.

"That's the first thing you need to know, where you can unbalance your opponent. For instance, which do you think is weaker, a guy's thighs or his knees?"

Robby and Max were both in their sweat clothes but had puffy jackets on over them. Robby kept putting his hands under his armpits and blowing on them. Max looked cold too.

They were standing in what Max said was a ready position, leaning forward from the hips with their arms forward, ready either to take advantage of the other guy's weak spots or to defend their own. Robby looked at Max and thought. "His knees, I think."

Max nodded. "Good. That's if you're facing him and he hasn't gotten hold of you somewhere. Check this out." Max fell onto one knee, reached around Robby's bent knees, and pulled them forward. Robby started to tip backward, but Max let go so he could right himself.

"Now try that with me, but try my thighs," Max directed.

They got back into ready position, and Robby went down onto one knee and put his arms around Max's thighs. Nothing happened.

"Hey, that's not easy," Robby protested.

"Exactly. Now try my knees."

This time Robby was able to make Max start to bend at the knees, but he suspected Max was letting him. "Now that was *too* easy."

Max grinned. "Don't worry. It won't always be. Now let's add my head in your belly."

He demonstrated, grabbing Robby's knees and pushing into his belly with his head, knocking him off his feet—almost.

Robby then got to try knocking Max back.

Max had Robby practice knee and leg takedowns for a while before moving on to a more complicated maneuver.

"Lean toward me," Max instructed Robby, but Max then grasped Robby's shoulders and pulled him toward himself. When Robby moved his leg forward, Max dropped to the playground surface on his knees.

"Whoa, what are you doing?" Robby protested breathlessly.

Max laughed. "Wrestling!" He had one knee behind Robby's lead foot. He put a hand behind Robby's forward leg and stood, pulling Robby's leg up into his armpit. Since Robby was standing with Max holding one leg up, it put him off balance.

"Now I reach around with my hand, like this, to the inside of your thigh." Max did just as he described. "And then I can turn and knock you on your butt." He at first kept Robby from falling, but the last attempt put Robby on his ass. "Ouch!" Robby protested. "I wasn't expecting that."

Max got back into ready stance after giving him a hand up. "You try it with me."

Robby stretched his shoulders to make himself ready and stepped toward Max. It took numerous tries with more explanation for Robby to get the sequence of motions, but he eventually had Max on his butt on the ground.

"This is fun!" Robby pronounced.

Max rubbed his butt and made a sour growling noise. "Maybe for you." But when Robby looked at him, he saw Max was grinning.

They tried a couple of other motions and then called it a day. Robby felt like he and Max had cemented a friendship, where in the past they had always been a bit distant. He high-fived him and waved as Max headed home.

ANDY KNOCKED on the exterior door of Robby's apartment on Saturday afternoon. He had some reference books with him, and they planned to practice building up knowledge for the Quiz Kids event that Monday.

Claire opened the door. "Oh, hi, it's you," she said.

Andy gave Robby's sister an amused look. "Yes, it's me. Hello, Claire. I'm here to practice Quiz Kids with Robby."

Claire just stood there, gazing at Andy. After a while she said, "I'm really sorry, you know. About what the boys did."

"Okay," Andy replied. "May I come in?"

Claire stepped back from the front door, looking flustered. "Oh, sorry." She watched Andy as he walked to the coat tree and hung up his hat and coat.

"What's it like?" Claire asked.

Andy stopped in the middle of stuffing his gloves in his coat pocket. "What's what like?" He knew full well what Claire was asking, but he wanted to make her say it.

"What's it like to be a girl who thinks she's a boy?"

Robby stood at the end of the entrance hall. "Claire!" he said ominously.

Claire jerked with surprise. "I'm just asking. What's wrong with that?"

"It's very rude," Robby said.

"Why?"

Andy waved a hand at Robby. "Forget it, dude. It doesn't mean anything. She's just asking."

Robby whirled to face Andy. "Well, she shouldn't ask. It's none of her business. It's your business, and that's what matters."

"Let's go to your room," Andy said.

Giving his sister a furious look, Robby nodded at Andy and led the way to his room. After he shut the door, he stood with his hands on his hips, looking hard at Andy. "Why do you let her get away with it?"

Sighing, Andy put his books on the computer desk. "Let's just get to work, can we?"

But Robby clearly wasn't ready to let the matter drop. "You let people walk all over you. You forgive the rudest behavior. You let those turds at school get away with murder. I bet you don't tell your parents what goes on. Why is that?"

Hanging his head, Andy walked to the bed and sat on the edge. "I don't want to talk about it."

Robby stared at him for a while. "I think kissing you makes it my business too."

Andy's head went up. "What?" he exclaimed.

85

Going over to the bed, Robby hesitated, then sat down next to Andy. He looked at his hands, fidgeting them in his lap. "I think you really like me. Like a boyfriend or something."

Andy could only stare at Robby, his mouth open. "A boyfriend?"

Putting his arm around Andy's shoulder, Robby gave him a squeeze. "Yeah, and I liked that. I want to be your... boyfriend."

Andy gazed into space in front of his eyes. He had liked Robby from the start, even entertained some mild fantasies about him. Andy had known he wasn't attracted to girls but was unsure how gay men might regard transmen as potential lovers. But what Robby was suggesting now suddenly opened a door for Andy to be the gay transman he knew he was. He responded with nervous hopefulness, "Does that mean you're gay or straight? I mean, if you really like me as Andy, then you're gay. But I don't have what it takes to be your boyfriend, down there. At least not yet."

"What, do you mean a penis? That doesn't matter to me."

Andy's face reddened. His disappointment was obvious. "Then that must mean you like me as a girlfriend, and I am *not* a girl."

Robby blanched at Andy's angry words. "I don't want you to be a girl," he said.

Andy glared at him. "Then what do you want?" His eyes blazed.

Robby looked long and hard at Andy. "I want *you*."

His mouth hanging open, Andy looked into Robby's eyes, allowing himself to hope. He leaned forward, and Robby put his mouth on Andy's. Andy felt his heart beat faster. Their tongues came out and explored each other's mouths. Andy, whose whole body was tingling with the contact with Robby's hard, firm front, almost trembled with excitement. He reached up and cupped Robby's cheek. They continued to kiss, and Andy stroked his cheek. Robby put his arms around Andy.

Andy could feel his body respond strongly to Robby's touch and kiss. Andy reached to cup Robby's asscheek and then let his hand come around and just lightly stroke the crotch of his jeans.

"Wait a minute," Andy cried, sitting up. "You aren't excited! You don't want me."

Robby wiped his mouth with the back of his hand and stared down at his lap. "I know. I don't know what's wrong with me. I can get excited. I can even whack off. But my dick isn't getting hard, and I know it should be."

Andy gazed at him, the side of his face very red and tears starting to form in his eyes. "It's okay, Robby. I understand. It's okay." But Andy knew Robby couldn't help but hear the anguish in his voice.

Robby threw him an angry look. "No, it's not okay. I'm eighteen years old. I have someone I care about in my arms. Why can't I get excited?"

Andy put his arm around Robby's shoulders and sighed. "And this doesn't happen with a girl? A real girl, I mean."

"You're a *real* girl!" Suddenly realizing what he'd said, Robby flushed as if embarrassed. "I didn't mean you *are* a girl. I just meant you're real… oh, damn it all to hell."

He jumped to his feet, but Andy grabbed his hand and dragged him down to the bed again. He pushed Robby on his back and stretched out beside him. He put his head on Robby's shoulder and his arm across his chest. "I know. I know. It's so fucked up."

Robby let his arm, now under Andy's body, bend until it settled around Andy's shoulders and hugged him. "I just wish I knew what was going on. With me, I mean."

"Shhh, shhhh," Andy soothed. "Just hold me." He was in a muddle over how to respond to this lovely boy. He knew he wanted him, but if Robby didn't feel the same, what did that mean? Did it mean that Robby's words weren't true? Andy felt all he could do was hold Robby and reassure him, whether that meant anything or not.

Robby held him.

THEY MUST have drifted off to sleep because they awoke when they heard Claire's voice. "What the...?" She stepped back from the door and called down the hall, "Mom! Robby's in bed with his girlfriend!"

Robby and Andy sat up and quickly smoothed down their hair. "Boyfriend," Robby corrected his sister. He glanced at Andy, and they both started to chuckle. They laughed harder. They both fell back on the bed clutching their bellies against the strength of their laughter.

Andy choked out, "Girlfriend!"

"Boyfriend!" laughed Robby.

They continued to lie back, holding each other and laughing. When their chuckles started to subside, they looked up to find Robby's mother standing in the bedroom doorway with her mouth open and Claire behind her shoulder, looking triumphant.

"I told you so!" she said to no one in particular.

Robby and Andy finally sat up, wiping their eyes. "That was wonderful," Andy said.

"I haven't laughed that hard since... since... well, I don't know." Robby gave his mother a frank look. "We were just kissing. Nothing more."

Andy gave him a *nothing more?* look, and they started to laugh again.

Robby's mother shook her head. "Keep the door open," she said, then pushed a protesting Claire down the hall.

"So...," Andy started slowly.

Robby looked at him and said, "So?"

With a mischievous look, Andy suggested, "Well, since we have to keep the door open, we probably should study for Quiz Kids."

Robby shrugged. "Makes sense. What are those books you brought?"

Andy climbed off the bed and picked up the books. "One of them is about astronomy. This one is about world cuisine. And this other one is about European history."

Robby looked at the books as Andy handed them to him. "And what are we going to do with them? We can hardly read them all."

Shrugging in return, Andy said, "We could quiz each other, and if we need to, one of us can read the book and teach the other."

Nodding regretfully that their affection had been stymied, Robby said, "Sounds good."

As Andy pulled out the desk chair and sat down, he turned to look at Robby to see his pensive look. "We'll get it figured out," he said reassuringly.

"What? How to study?"

"No. Why you aren't getting excited."

"Oh. Okay." Robby placed his hand on Andy's shoulder. "It can't be as hard as Quiz Kids."

Andy smirked. "From your mouth to God's ear."

CHAPTER 11

THE FIRST competition for Quiz Kids was the following Monday, and both Robby and Andy were excited. It would be televised as usual on the school district's cable channel. They got a ride to the studio from Mr. and Mrs. Kahn, who would be in the audience. Robby's mother said she would wait to watch the competition when it was made available to parents. Needless to say, Robby was disappointed about that. He couldn't help but see how much Andy's mother and father supported him, while his own mother seemed always distracted. He realized he hadn't thought all that much about it since he was younger, but watching the Kahns made it start to hurt.

The man who directed the competition greeted the two boys and Andy's parents when they arrived in the cramped studio at the school building. He seemed harried and rushed but tried to be gracious. Mrs. Kahn fussed over Robby and Andy, and the director seemed more bothered than pleased. Luis had caught a ride with them and grinned at Andy when his mother made such a big deal about him. The two boys were so nervous they didn't really mind.

Andy elbowed Robby as the director explained the rules of the competition. "I wonder if any of my old schoolmates from Olympia will be watching."

Robby looked at him and shook his head. "This is King County. Olympia is in Thurston. I doubt their cable company even has our shows."

"Oh. Of course," Andy said. "I hadn't thought of that. I suppose they won't see us until, or if, we make the state finals."

"We will," Robby said, grinning.

"Cool," said Andy without conviction.

Robby was surprised at Andy's reaction, but just then they were herded into their places behind the two sets of desks and he didn't have time to think about it.

The emcee was a teacher from a high school in Issaquah and looked to be in his early forties but neat and trim. He had a good speaking voice and introduced all the contestants from Highlands View High and Eastlake High. He also introduced the alternates and the scorekeeper and judge, a rather humorless-looking teacher from Redmond.

Then the competition got underway. The questions covered the scholastic board, from literature to geography to history to biology and more. The teams knew their members' areas of expertise. When a question came up in one of them, the members would turn to the teen who knew that topic and he or she would supply the answer. The system worked well, so long as another team member didn't try to overrule the subject expert.

Andy was a specialist in literature and also math. Robby knew math as well but also the other sciences. The other two members of the team were a junior named Mark Hamilton and a senior named Bella Bianchi. Mark knew history, and Bella knew her arts. They were well balanced, and no one seemed to think he or she knew more than they did.

The first questions were toss-ups that either team could answer. The emcee asked, "They say curiosity killed the cat. It did not help this mythological person either, who received gifts from all the gods. She was given a box that—"

Someone from Eastlake hit their buzzer first. As one of the girls from that school answered "Pandora," Robby realized he would have answered, "Who is Pandora?" He had to remember this wasn't *Jeopardy!* and that answers didn't need to be in the form of a question. He chuckled under his breath.

The second question was "This novelist was born in India. He fought in the Spanish Civil War, and his novel *1984* predicted a grim future."

Andy had his finger on the buzzer first. "Andrew Kahn for Highlands View High," called the emcee.

Andy said, "George Orwell."

"Correct!" said the emcee.

Robby grinned and nodded to Andy, who smiled shyly back.

The first set of questions in the toss-up round continued. One question asked about a president who fought in the War of 1812, the Blackhawk War, and the Mexican War; ran as a Whig; died of gastroenteritis; and was succeeded by his vice president, Millard Fillmore, got a wrong answer from a boy on the Eastlake team. "Franklin Pierce."

"That is incorrect," said the emcee.

Highlands View's Mark hit his buzzer and answered, "William Henry Harrison."

The correct answer was Zachary Taylor.

More questions came up about the Quakers, Upton Sinclair, and a Scottish engineer whose last name was chosen to refer to a measurement of energy at the rate of one joule per second. Robby buzzed in for that one, correctly answering "James Watt" and congratulating himself again that he hadn't said "Who is...." He could hear one of the members on Eastlake team groaning and sighing when they got questions wrong. He counseled himself to keep mum and just answer when he could.

The competition went by so fast that Andy sounded breathless when he answered a question about a Shakespearean play set on a magical island with *The Tempest*.

Robby shook his head at how badly the other team did when the emcee announced a lightning round. All the characters were in novels even he easily could have identified, but the other team only got one correct, *The Great Gatsby*'s Daisy Buchanan. When it was Highlands View's turn to try, Andy answered all but one of the characters, Jack Dawkins, better known as the Artful Dodger in *Oliver Twist*.

But when Highlands View got a lightning round about US history, Robby misunderstood one of the questions. He thought the emcee said "1864" in a question about the Voting Rights Act and got a hateful stare from Mark when he answered "Abraham Lincoln" instead of Lyndon Johnson.

They were all cross and breathless at the end. The last question was about a state which entered the union in 1845, whose state flower was the bluebonnet, and which had just increased its speed limit statewide to eighty-five. The Eastlake High team member who buzzed in said "Oregon." Mark took it for Highlands View with "Texas." The emcee gave the final score, Highlands View with 230 and Eastlake with 95. They had won and would face the next high school in a week.

Afterward the Kahns took Andy, Luis and Robby out for ice cream at Dairy Queen, where they ordered Peanut Buster Parfaits. They were punch-drunk and got hysterical quoting the donkey in *Shrek* about how nobody doesn't like parfaits. They couldn't stop laughing, and Mr. Kahn finally made them leave the Dairy Queen. Robby and Andy hung on each other all the way back to Robby's place.

When Robby got inside, his mother was gone, and Claire wouldn't answer her locked bedroom door. He sighed and headed to his bedroom. He texted Andy and told him he was awesome and that he thought he loved him.

When Andy texted back that he definitely loved Robby, Robby realized he and his friend were in danger of taking their relationship to a serious level. He didn't know how he felt about that. He didn't know if Andy knew what he might be getting in for. For that matter, neither did he.

THAT MONDAY at school, Luis, Max, and Rhonda were the only classmates who knew anything about the Quiz Kids competition. They congratulated Andy and Robby. A couple of the teachers did too.

Robby was nervous around Andy, watching him to see if he had taken the text conversation too seriously, but Andy was his usual sardonically humorous self. Robby decided not to sweat it, though he did find a chance to talk quietly with Max.

"Do you think Andy is, um, into me?"

Max stopped walking and looked at him. "Do you think he is?" he asked.

"I dunno."

Max gazed at Robby speculatively. "How about you? Are you into him?"

Robby didn't answer right away. He was thinking about his own lack of response to either boys or girls, and he finally said, "I dunno that either."

Max's eyebrows went up. Robby noticed Max was eyeing him speculatively, even with interest. *I wonder if he is getting into me?* he thought. "Hey, we missed wrestling lessons Saturday so you could practice for your competition. We still on for this weekend?"

Robby thought about it. "I guess so. The taping isn't until 8:00 p.m., so we could get together earlier in the day."

"You're taping again this weekend? Oh yeah, you guys won. Who you going up against this time?"

Shrugging, Robby admitted, "I haven't heard who won the other round."

Max waited for him to say more. Then he asked again, "Well, how about 10:00 a.m. for your next lesson?"

Distracted, Robby said, "Yeah, sure. That should work."

IT OCCURRED to Robby that he hadn't heard from his Aunt Ivy in a couple of weeks, and he decided to go over to her place that evening. When she answered the door, she was all smiles.

"Nothing else missing?" he asked her.

"Oh yes," she said with a shrug. "Lots of things. But I decided since they always turn up later, it must be my brain going. I just misplace things and then eventually put them back. Come in and have some tea and cake."

He followed her through the cluttered foyer and down the hall to the kitchen. "What's been missing?"

She walked to the stove and turned on the burner under the tea kettle, then went to the refrigerator and took out a cake with several slices already gone. "Oh, this and that. Nothing important."

Robby didn't know what to say. He had never really thought someone was stealing from his aunt, but then again, he and Andy had started to believe her after her trip to the hospital. "Are you sure, Aunt Ivy? They said your brain was fine."

He sat at the table as she laid out a small plate with a piece of German chocolate cake on it and retrieved a teacup from the cabinet. She set milk and sugar on the table too.

"Oh, I don't know. You can be absentminded without having anything organically wrong with your brain. I bought some new things I want to show you. I found them at a junk shop. Some really quite lovely things."

Robby accepted the cup of tea and started to put sugar and milk in it. He picked up his fork. "I don't think you'll ever stop collecting all these things, will you?"

She leveled a look of mischievous glee at him. "Never, never, never."

They wandered into her office after they had eaten and cleared away the things. On her desk were some small items, the usual treasures Ivy would find. Robby went over and picked one up. They were a set of postcards, old photography of a Midwestern-looking city. He turned the packet over and saw the legend. "World's Columbian Exhibition, Chicago, 1893."

"Aren't those beautiful? It was quite the exposition. The Columbian they called it. It was supposed to be the 400th anniversary of Columbus discovering America. Sort of poetic, it being in 1893 instead of 1892, given that Columbus didn't discover America at all. He didn't even think he did."

She took the packet from his hand and removed the rubber band that held them together. She selected one and showed it to him. "They called it the White City because of all the white marble classical buildings. Of course, they weren't made of marble, except the one that is still there. They were just painted boards. But not too many people know that before the Columbian Exposition the grand buildings, city halls, museums, weren't made like that. It was revolutionary and set the model for decades. Good old Daniel Burnham and Frederick Law Olmsted, the designers."

Robby looked at the postcards one by one. "What did you mean about Columbus not discovering America? You mean like the Vikings or the Indians or something?"

She looked at him for a moment, gathering her thoughts. "Oh well, yes, them, but also Columbus had charts, in Spanish or Portuguese, I think, so he obviously was hardly the first person to set foot on the continent. Even among Italian explorers." She took a new tack. "Did you know that all that about no one knowing Leif Eriksson was here is also nonsense? The Vatican has record of a Bishop of Vinland and Thule from before Columbus was even born. What I don't understand is why we continue to believe things that just aren't true. Like how everyone thought the Earth was flat. All you have to do is look at the ocean and you can see the surface of the Earth is curved."

Good old Aunt Ivy always had some provocative new information or theory about history and geography. Robby loved being around her.

"What's this?" he asked, reaching for a box that looked big enough for a large alarm clock.

She reached to take it from his hand. "I don't know. They were thinking of just tossing it away, but I made them sell it to me for a dollar." She opened the cardboard box to reveal a wooden box inside. She had Robby help her pry out the inner box. He put the wooden box on the desk and tried to open it.

"Is there some kind of trick to this?" he asked.

His aunt just wiggled her shoulders, which she did when she was impatient for someone else to figure something out.

Robby sat down on the desk chair and started to examine the box. It appeared to be made of some pale wood, though it was amply stained. If there had been any sort of label, it had long come off. There seemed to be a paler part of the wood where a label might have been. He reached into his pocket for his Swiss Army knife and pulled out a tool he could use to try to pry the box open.

"Be careful!" Aunt Ivy's voice came out a little shrill, again a habit of hers when someone else was investigating one of her treasures.

He put his tongue between his teeth as he poked here and there. He was unable to find a place where the tip of his tool would separate the pieces of wood. He tried other angles. Then he must have pressed some sort of latch because the whole box burst open. The bottom and back remained in a piece, but the top and sides fell away, though still attached. He realized as he took the thing in his hands that the top and sides would come away from the bottom and back if he slid them forward and up. They were attached by grooves where they could be inserted again.

"Oh my word!" Aunt Ivy exclaimed.

Inside the box was some sort of mechanism. It was old and tarnished, almost rusted if it had originally been made of iron or steel. It was roughly round, with bits of metal ornaments all around it. The paint, most likely enamel, was covered in a layer of black grime. There were protuberances that could have been ornament or even controls.

"Now what do you suppose that is?" Ivy asked.

"I have no idea. It looks old, though."

Ivy looked at Robby and said, "Do you think so?"

He shrugged. "Let's get Andy to come over and look at it. Maybe his mom or dad would have an idea what it is."

WHEN ROBBY got home that evening, he called Andy and told him about the mysterious device.

"What do you think it is?" Andy asked.

"A music box? Maybe a little automaton? Or it could just be a paperweight."

"What is your aunt Ivy going to do with it?"

"I don't know. I suggested getting it appraised, but she dismissed that. She said, 'What if it's just junk?'"

"True," Andy said. "You know, *Antiques Roadshow* might be coming here. Let me look it up on the KUOW website and find out."

"That's a great idea! If nothing else, it'll be fun." Robby smiled broadly. They had a plan.

CHAPTER 12

THE KAHNS asked to take Robby out to a late lunch on Saturday, but he thanked them and declined. He was going to Max's and knew he would be sweaty afterward and would need to get dressed. He showed up at Max's at about 10:00 a.m. in his torn sweatpants and a sleeveless sweatshirt in spite of the fact it was a chilly February in the Puget Sound region.

He rang the doorbell and was let in by a younger child to a house full of toys and kids' clothing and a whole lineup of shoes haphazardly tossed about by the front door. He stood, unsure if he were expected to take off his shoes, but then he saw a pile of what must be cat barf on the carpet and decided not. Nevertheless he walked carefully to avoid stepping in something. He hadn't realized Max had so many sisters and brothers. It was a good-sized house but probably didn't have any more than three bedrooms. His own apartment had that many.

He saw a girl he recognized come and peer into the entranceway at him. She was Tina, a freshman. He lifted his hand in greeting and got a nod back. "I'm here for Max," he explained.

Max loped into the hallway just minutes later, pulling on a windbreaker. "Let's use the garage. It's cold outside."

Opening the garage door revealed a car already in the garage. Max swore and went back into the house, saying, "I'll get someone to move that."

Robby watched while Max's dad came out, pulling on a shirt, and moved the two cars in the driveway before parking the car from the garage in their place. Just as he turned off the ignition, another car pulled in behind him. A high-school-age boy got out and greeted Max and his dad. Max informed Robby, "This is Jim, Tina's boyfriend."

Robby wondered what it would be like to have so many people in and out of the house all the time. While they were exchanging greetings, an older man came out of the house and shook Jim's hand. "That's my grandpa," Max explained.

The two boys went into the garage now that the car was out. Max started moving all sorts of things out of the way: boxes, bikes, trikes, kids' toys, a couple of laundry baskets full of clothes, a car mechanic's toolbox, and numerous unidentifiable items. He then shut the garage door. "It's cold," he explained, then grabbed a push broom.

"Let me do that," Robby offered.

Max gave him the broom and watched as he swept the floor. When he had the floor clear, Max found a wrestling mat somewhere and dragged it out.

"I'm going to knock you on your back," he said, grinning at Robby. "Get into your ready stance."

Robby complied, facing Max. He crouched and put his arms out. Max was already in position.

"I'm going to make you think I'm going to put you in a fireman's carry, maybe a choke hold or inside trip."

In the intervening weeks, Max had taught Robby all these holds, so he knew what to expect.

Max leaned forward, grabbed one of Robby's shoulders, and put the other hand on the back of his neck. He started to turn him clockwise so Robby had to step around him. Suddenly, on the second turn, Max stepped into him and put his knee between Robby's legs, pushed, and tripped him. Robby found himself on the mat with Max on his knee leaning over him.

"Ha! That's a neat trick!" Robby laughed breathlessly.

"Now you try it," Max said.

After three tries Robby had Max on the floor. He was so winded he stayed above Max. Max's face was tight. He struggled to shift so Robby's knee was away from his groin.

His voice was choked when he said, "Let's try something new."

Max approached Robby in a starting stance, as if gauging for where he could get a good hold on him. In spite of Max looking here and there to choose his attack, Robby noticed Max was a little red-faced and wouldn't look him in the eye. The exertion, looking for a hold lower on his torso, that would all explain it.

Max lunged forward and took Robby's shoulder in a tight grip. He tried to get one foot behind Robby's knee, but Robby managed to prevent him this time. He tried another hold, reaching around Robby to grab a thigh from behind, but he missed his chance, and Robby stepped back. Max's face had an intense expression, his mouth open.

Suddenly Max stepped forward and took Robby in his arms. He pressed his lips on Robby's, then tried to push his tongue in between Robby's teeth. Robby could feel Max's erection digging into his belly. He was so startled, he just let it happen. He didn't open his mouth, but he let Max kiss him.

Max quickly pulled away and wiped his lips with the back of his hand. "I'm sorry. I'm sorry." His face was really red now. "I thought…. I mean…. You seemed…. I wanted to…."

Robby realized Max was in fact, as he had suspected, gay. "No, really. It's okay. I just…." He was glad the garage door was shut, since he could hear kids' voices on the driveway.

Max stood with his arms hanging at his sides. He looked truly miserable. He had tears in his eyes. "This is really bogus."

"No," Robby said again. "It's okay. Really. I didn't mind. I was just surprised."

Max had turned away, but now he looked back. "Huh?" he said, truly puzzled. "I thought, with you going to PFLAG and hanging with Andy and all that…. And you never did anything to discourage me. And I was starting to get into you."

"I know, I know. I… I don't know if I'm gay or straight, so if you thought I was gay, well, you might be right."

Max went back to standing close to his friend. "I might be right?"

Now it was Robby's turn to feel miserable. "I honestly don't know what's wrong with me. I mean, I buffed up to see if getting all masculine would make something happen, but now I've kissed a girl and a boy and nothing…."

Max's face was a picture of befuddlement. "What are you saying?"

Robby gave him an intense look of appeal. "Nothing happens when I kiss someone. Nothing at all."

Max put one forearm on Robby's shoulder. He leaned in and said against his lips, "Well, maybe you just didn't give it a chance." He put his lips to Robby's and waited for him to open his mouth to let Max's tongue in.

Robby thought, *Even if I am into men, how will I know if I'm into Max?* He didn't especially like the taste of Max's mouth. It was like some overly fruit-flavored gum. He finally pushed Max away with the heels of his hands on Max's shoulders.

"No, Max, no. It's not working."

Max stepped back. "So you're not gay," he stated.

"I don't know. I don't think so. But I don't think I'm straight either. I kissed Andy, and that did nothing for me either."

He realized after he said it that he had just completely confused the situation. Max didn't know that Andy had a girl's body. He was looking at Robby now as if he was raving. "Oh Christ," Robby said. He looked at Max. "Wanna go get a soda or something?"

"I'd really like a beer," Max replied. "We can get one inside. I share my room with two of my brothers. What if we go into the backyard and sit on the swings?"

Thinking that not having a large family wasn't so bad after all, Robby nodded. "Would you get the beers and meet me back there?"

Max went through a door directly into the kitchen. Robby looked around and saw a door that looked like it led into a backyard. Once out on the patio, he found he first had to navigate the toys and bicycles; then when he stepped on the grass, which was dry, yellow, and sparse, he just missed stepping into a pile of dog shit. He finally made his way to a rickety set of swings in the back. When he sat on one, he almost lost his balance.

Max came out the back door and picked his way to Robby. He sat on the swing next to him after handing him a Budweiser.

Robby twisted off the cap and took a long swallow. They sat a few minutes in silence. Robby could hear Max's little sisters and brothers both in the house and in the front yard laughing, screaming, and a little one crying.

"Where do I start?" he asked rhetorically.

Max laughed gruffly. "How about what you said about Andy."

Robby groaned inwardly. "I'm not turning out to be a very good confidant. I've outed him twice now."

Max took a slug of his beer and sat forward, his elbows on his knees. He looked up and sideways at Robby. "So the secret is that Andy is really a girl? I knew that. Everybody at school knows that."

Robby found he wanted to argue that Andy was a boy, that he just had a girl's body, but then he shrugged. "So... you know he was born a girl. He figured out he was a boy a couple of years ago, or rather he always knew he was a boy, but he finally told his parents, and they're very supportive."

After a moment Max asked, "So is she... is *he* having surgery?"

"He already had some. He doesn't know if he'll go all the way. You know, and have a penis made." His face was coloring at the private nature of what he was disclosing. "But this is all terribly secret. You know that, I hope."

"Oh yeah, I'm not going to tell anyone. I have my own secrets." Max took another swig and gave Robby a sardonic look. "So is he the 'girl' you kissed?"

Robby felt miserable. He knew that if Andy knew he was talking about this, he would be furious. "I shouldn't say any more. But yes, kinda."

"Kinda? Did you kiss or not?" Max said exasperated.

"Yeah, we did."

"And?"

Looking over at Max briefly, Robby shrugged. "Nothing."

Max sat up and stared at him. He demanded, "What do you mean 'nothing'?"

"It's complicated. I just didn't get aroused. My… um… dick didn't react at all." Robby was sure his face was now beet red.

Max sat forward again, this time with only one elbow on his knee. "But couldn't that be because you know he's a girl?"

Robby chuckled. "But he's not a girl. He's a boy."

Max gazed at him for a while, then sighed. "And with me… nothing then either?"

"No," Robby said miserably.

Again they sat for some time. They heard the back door open and saw Tina look out at them, then turn around and go back in. Max said, hesitatingly, "So you never get a boner?"

"Oh, I do. I can jerk off. I don't picture anyone when I do that, though. Or if I do, it doesn't make it any better or hotter. It's really strange."

Max got up and walked to a garbage can. He opened it and tossed his empty beer bottle into it. Robby found himself absurdly thinking *Isn't he going to recycle that?*

Max picked his way back, checking the bottom of his shoe once. It was clean. He walked up to where Robby was sitting and said, "So it's not that you're not gay, but that you aren't anything. You just don't feel anything for me or anyone. Man, that's bogus. What are you going to do?"

Robby looked up at his friend and gave him a lost look. "I don't know if there is anything I can do."

Later that evening, Robby found it difficult to concentrate on the competition.

Andy kept looking at him strangely. "What's eating you, bro?" he asked.

"I don't want to talk about it."

His brow knitted, Andy said, "Well, all right. Maybe later?"

"Maybe later."

CHAPTER 13

AUNT IVY had the little device, or so it proved to be, cleaned by a neighborhood teen boy who had cars he was fixing and had all the solvents and rags he needed. She called Robby to come over when the boy delivered it back to her. "You won't believe how beautiful it is."

When he arrived at her door, he found it unlocked. He went in and walked up to her office.

"Robby, look at this lovely thing!" Aunt Ivy crowed.

"Aunt Ivy, you need to start locking your doors. Someone could come in and steal something or attack you." It was an old argument they had, and as always, Aunt Ivy ignored him.

"There's nothing worth stealing in here, and who would attack a decrepit old woman?" she said.

His eyes lit onto the device, now shiny and clean, in an honored position on her desk. It looked like an egg with four little legs and lots of decorations on it. The surface was a deep red with gold and white flowers, tiny ones, going up the sides and around the middle. It had little gold fleurs-de-lis stamped on the red enamel.

"Look what it does!" Aunt Ivy said. She took the top and bottom in her hands and opened the egg by pressing a latch that was hidden in the gold filigree around its middle. It popped open and

106

revealed a tiny ballerina inside. She started to turn on a mirrored base, while a music box played a little tune Robby didn't recognize. The interior of the egg was lined with some sort of gold satin.

"How did that satin manage not to get really filthy?" Robby asked.

Aunt Ivy shrugged. "The egg was airtight."

"Huh," he said. "What is that melody?"

She shook her head.

"It sounds familiar somehow," Robby said absently. He picked it up and turned it this way and that. He found the hole where a key would be inserted to wind the music box spring. "Did you find a key?"

Aunt Ivy looked at him. "No, there wasn't one, but we found something else that worked. And I don't know what the song is. I think it might be Tchaikovsky, but I can't place it. I don't know all his works."

Robby continued to examine the egg. "You know, Aunt Ivy, that PBS show *Antiques Roadshow* will be in Tacoma next month. We should take the egg there and see if it's worth anything."

Aunt Ivy had a dreamy look in her eyes when she nodded to Robby. "That's a good idea," she said.

He called Andy on his cell phone. "You should go ahead and sign up for *Antiques Roadshow*. I think Aunt Ivy might have something here."

"Can I come look at it?" he asked.

"Sure. Can you come over today?"

Andy hesitated. "I have to help Mom with something, but I can ask her to drop me over after that."

Nearly two hours later, Andy was at the door. Robby had locked it when he arrived, so he had to go answer it.

"Hey, Andy, come upstairs and see this thing. Aunt Ivy has it in her office."

The two trudged up the stairs and into Ivy's little office. They found her on her computer looking at other eggs.

"Are you finding anything, Aunt Ivy?" Robby asked her.

She put up one finger to indicate "Just one minute," then read something to herself and slowly turned. She started to speak but froze when she saw Andy's face. "What is it, dear?" she asked.

Andy's eyes were wide open and his mouth round in an astounded *O*. He came forward to where the egg sat on the desk to the right of the mouse pad. He reached for it, then stopped and asked, "May I?"

Ivy nodded and said, "Of course, dear." She watched as Andy gingerly picked up the egg and looked at it.

Ivy reached up and pressed the spring latch. The egg came open, the ballerina started to spin, and the music started.

"Ohhhh…" came from Andy's open lips. He listened for a few moments. "That's the waltz from *Yevgeny Onegin*! By Tchaikovsky. It's tinny, so it doesn't convey the richness of the full orchestra, but I'm sure that's it."

"When was that written? The waltz, I mean?" Robby took the music box from Andy's hand and looked to see if a date was inscribed anywhere.

Andy frowned. "I don't know, maybe the late 1870s or 1880s. He died in 1893 of cholera."

Robby looked at him quizzically. "How come you know so much?"

"He's my mother's favorite composer. You know, he was gay."

"Who isn't?" Robby jested.

Andy looked at him expectantly, but Robby didn't explain. "Well, the date of the music doesn't tell us a thing," Ivy interrupted. "Once a piece of music is written, it can be added to something at any time. The egg could be from Imperial Russia, or it could be from the 1960s."

The two boys nodded sagely.

"That's why we need to take this on *Antiques Roadshow*," said Robby.

"It sure looks like an Imperial Egg by Fabergé," Andy observed.

Both Robby and Ivy chorused, "No!"

"It can't be. It's just a reproduction or a fake or something," Ivy pronounced.

"Like I said, that's why we need to take this on the show," said Robby again.

ANDY TURNED to Ivy. "Mrs. Beaumont? May I ask you a question?"

Ivy looked back at him. "Well, of course you can. And that's Ivy, not Mrs. Beaumont. What is it, young man?"

Smiling discreetly at Ivy's use of "young man," which never failed to please him, Andy asked, "Were you ever married? Do you have any children? I've never heard Robby mention any cousins, not by you anyway."

Ivy stopped fiddling with the device and put her forefinger to her chin. She smiled, remembering something lovely. "Why, yes, my dear. I was married. For over thirty years to a wonderful man named Ernest. That's what he was, earnest. But no children. We always had cats. Mr. Duck was just a kitten when Ernest passed away. I think sometimes his sweet, loving nature is a remnant of Ernest's spirit." Her eyes grew pensive. "What a good, sweet man he was. He was ill for much of the end of his too-short life. We slept in separate bedrooms toward the end because of it. I didn't want to be parted from Ernest, but he insisted. I wanted to keep him at home, so I retired from teaching to look after him."

Andy realized Ernest's bedroom must be the closed door at the end of the hall that Robby had never invited him into. He wanted to reach out and touch Ivy on the arm but held back. "How long ago did he…?"

Ivy looked into his eyes and smiled impishly. "Die? You can say that word in this house. He died just eight years ago. I went into his room in the morning to find he had passed peacefully in his sleep.

Mr. Duck was snuggled in between his legs. He, the cat I mean, looked up at me as I came in, a puzzled look on his face, like he was saying, 'Something's wrong with Dad.' I realized Ernest was gone." She looked over to where Mr. Duck was sitting in the doorway of her office. "I went over to give Ernest one last little peck on the lips. Mr. Duck got up and snuggled on his still chest. He is such a kissy duck, er, I mean cat. But this time he just looked at Ernest's face. Then he looked up at mine, and I leaned over to let him press his forehead to mine, the way he kisses. Mr. Duck, I mean. Then he got down and went off to find a nice warm cat bed to sleep in."

Now Andy did put his hand on Ivy's arm. "Oh, Ivy, I'm so sorry."

Ivy's eyes took on a light from within. "You shouldn't be. We had so many years together with our many cats. Our marriage went through all the phases it could, from early adventures abroad to sitting quietly and holding hands. The night before he died, he asked me if I regretted anything at all in my life. I laughed and told him that I only regretted saying good-bye to all our cats over the years. I asked him the same. He said, 'Not a thing, and I'll tell all those cats how much you loved them when I see them again in the Summerland.'"

"Summerland?"

Ivy put a hand to Andy's cheek. "We were never Christians, in spite of my working all those years for the archdiocese. The Summerland is from older traditions, where people and animals are together and there is no war, no hunger, no jealousy, no differences between races or religions or genders or anything. I hope someday when I die, I will find Ernest and all our cats there waiting for me."

Andy stood, his mouth hanging open, so moved by this representation that when Robby came back in, he asked, "What happened? What did I miss?"

Andy and Ivy both smiled at him. "Nothing," they chorused.

Robby looked from one to the other, then shrugged. "Whatever," he said.

ANDY FOUND instructions online to request tickets for a taping of the *Antiques Roadshow* on May 15. They filled out the applications online, and Aunt Ivy checked the box to indicate she had a piece to be appraised. She smiled and said, "Now we wait for a postcard saying they are interested in my egg."

In the meantime the Highlands View High Quiz Kids team was scheduled for its last competition. They had one by one beaten every other high school in the district, then the county, and now they were going to state trials. It would also be held in April in Olympia.

"Now I can start worrying about my old classmates recognizing me," Andy shared.

"What's the likelihood?"

Andy shrugged. "I guess we'll see."

Robby looked at his friend, feeling the emotions he always inspired these days—affection and a little protectiveness, like he was a big brother.

He reached for Andy's shoulder and squeezed it. "If anyone says anything, they'll have to answer to me."

Giving him an amused smirk, Andy said "Oh, big tough man, champion for all the oppressed."

They spent every evening together, either at Robby's, Andy's, or Aunt Ivy's house, studying for the final event. Aunt Ivy's house was a mixed blessing. She could be quite a distraction, bringing over new treasures she'd found and expounding at length on their historical significance. On the other hand, she seemed to know everything. When either Robby quizzed Andy, or Andy was the one who asked a question about science, history, literature or some other likely Quiz Kids question, Aunt Ivy's voice would come through from another room with the correct answer. At first it was okay; then it started to get irritating. Finally they would both stop, look over their shoulders, wait for Ivy's answer, then fall into laughter at how reliable she was.

Mr. Duck stuck close to them whenever they were at Ivy's house. He was even waiting by the door one time when they arrived. He would follow them either to the parlor or the kitchen, find a place to station himself on another chair, and seem to be listening while they discussed a question.

Robby found the time he spent with Andy was the most comfortable and rewarding of his life. He enjoyed spending time at Andy's house, with Mrs. Kahn always coming in with cookies or cake and Mr. Kahn's proud smile when he looked at his son. Even Gabe was a treat, looking in with some joke or another about what they were studying. He could see how Andy got so smart and so clever.

After studying they would have a cup of herbal tea and talk. Or, if they'd been studying at Aunt Ivy's, he would walk Andy home and hold his hand. The shy smiles back and forth were among the sweetest things about their time together.

That is, until one evening when they approached Andy's condo and didn't notice a car running its engine across the street.

"Look at the faggots holding hands!" came a boy's voice from the open front window of the car.

"They can't be faggots, because Andrea's a he-she," said another boy from the backseat.

"Oh for God's sake," Andy lamented. "You'd think after most of a school year, they'd have gotten something new to do or been expelled or something."

Robby glared furiously at the car. "That's enough!" he declared, dropping Andy's hand to stride across the street.

"Robby, no!" Andy cried.

Robby went to the front window of the car and found himself looking straight into the sneering face of Smartass.

"Ooh, it's lover boy. Found what Andy has in his shorts yet?"

Robby stood with his hands on his hips. "Look, Bradley, I don't know what it is you have between your ears, but you probably should demand your money back. It's pretty pathetic."

One of Smartass's friends, Grease, said from the open back window, "That's more than you have in your pants!"

Robby leaned over to peer into the car. "Claire, are you in there?"

There was no answer, but while he was leaning over, Smartass reached out, grabbed his collar, and pulled him forward so he struck his head on the window frame.

"Cut that out!" came a grown man's voice. Andy had gone into his condo and told his father what was happening outside. "I called the cops. They'll be here any minute."

Grease said, "Shit, let's go."

Smartass said, "You gonna let this kike scare you?"

Grease answered, "No, but I'm gonna let my dad scare me out of a trip to Disneyland if I get busted."

Smartass relented, spit on Robby, and put his foot to the accelerator and took off.

Mr. Kahn said, "Charming." As he led Andy and Robby back to the other side of the street, he added, "Your principal will get an earful about this—"

"No, Dad," Andy interrupted. "You don't understand. If they know you ratted on them, Robby and I will get our asses kicked at school."

Mr. Kahn turned to his son and said severely, "Andrew, you can't let bullies like that control you."

"I can if they outnumber me."

Robby watched Mr. Kahn and Andy spar about the hoods who had been taunting them.

"They're all talk. They're just trying to piss us off. They aren't going to do anything dangerous." Andy's desperation was palpable.

His father was adamant. "That's the sort of thinking that got Jews killed by the millions in Nazi Germany." In a singsong voice, he mimicked, "They won't hurt any Jews. They just like to paint slogans on shop windows and put dead cats on your doorstep."

Andy rolled his eyes. "Dad!" he protested.

Robby started to back away. "I should get home," he said.

Mr. Kahn looked over at him and then back at Andy. "You should go inside too. I'll talk to you in the morning."

Andy gave Robby a long-suffering look and went into the condo. His father, after a quick good-bye to Robby, followed him.

Back at their apartment, Robby checked to see if Claire was home. She was. She answered the knock on her bedroom door with "Yeah?"

He pushed the door open and stepped inside. "You weren't with Smartass and his boys tonight, eh?"

She leveled a resentful look at him. "That's none of your business."

"As long as they torment Andy, it's my business."

She had been sitting at her computer playing *Bubble Shooter*, but now she closed the program and turned around to face him in her chair, her arms crossed over her chest. "Oh, are you Andy's keeper?"

He glared at his sister. "I just have to stick up for him. Your buddies not only called him a faggot, but a kike tonight."

"What's that got to do with me?" she challenged.

"Just think about who your friends are. I don't think Mom would—"

"Oh, Mom Shmom. You've just got a boner for that freak. You fly off the handle if anyone so much as questions what he—what she is. All the special provisions they had to make at school for her. Separate showers, a different rule about swimwear in gym. Everyone carefully watching which gender pronoun they use about… *it*. I swear, people like that want the world just so they can play their little dress-up games."

Robby was floored by his sister's vehemence. "Wow, where did all that come from?"

She whirled on him from where she had turned to her monitor again. "You! That's where. You used to be so quiet and nice. Now I feel like the Inquisition is always at my door."

"If you chose better company—"

"You should talk!" she screeched at him. "Now get out! I don't want to talk to you."

She came over and physically shoved him out her door, slammed it, and locked it behind him. He thought he probably should have told her Mr. Kahn was calling the police. *Ah, to hell with her.* Too bad if she got arrested again.

"Robby, do you have a safe at your house?" Aunt Ivy asked him a couple of days later.

"No, we don't. What do you need it for?" he inquired of her.

"We have one," said Andy, who had come over to his aunt's house with Robby.

Aunt Ivy brought over the small wooden box the music-box egg was kept in. "Can you put this in there until the day of the *Roadshow*? I would feel a lot better."

Robby grinned. "So now you think the thing is valuable?"

"No, not really, but I just have a feeling…."

"What sort of feeling, Ivy?" Andy asked her, putting a hand gently on her arm.

Ivy gave him a grateful smile. "That someone wants it, and I want to find out about it before… well, before it disappears."

The two boys exchanged looks.

"Aunt Ivy, has anyone said anything or shown special interest in the egg or anything?" Robby was concerned.

"No, not really. Like I said, it's just a feeling."

"Okay, I'll take it home and put it in our safe. Dad will have to open it for me, but he's reliable." Andy took the box and put it in his backpack.

"I'll give you a ride home," Robby offered. "I've got the car this evening."

"Oh, is your sister in trouble again?" Aunt Ivy asked. "I don't know what's gotten into that girl. She was always so sweet and polite."

"No, I just asked for the car, and she didn't need it tonight."

Robby waited for Ivy to leave the room and asked, "So, did your dad call the principal?"

Andy sighed deeply. "Yes, he did. I'm afraid to go to school. He called the police too, but they just blew him off. I don't think the principal did anything either."

Andy looked down. "I don't know. I know I told my dad that I thought they were all talk, but I'm not really so sure. They almost pantsed me that time. That was a long time ago, but the looks I get from Smartass really scare me sometimes. He likes to come up to me and rub his groin on my butt. And he's felt for my boobs when we're in the locker room. I don't know if he's a perv. There's just something—not right about that dude."

"Well, one good thing," Robby said.

"That is?"

"I don't think Claire is hanging out with them anymore. I noticed she's always home, always studying. I've had the car a lot lately. Mom is pleased. She—I mean Claire—tore me a new one the other day, but though she would never admit it, I think she's had quite enough of her lowlife friends."

MR. KAHN showed a lot of interest in the music box when he took it from Andy to put into their little safe on the floor of his den. "It's exquisite! Where did she say she got it?"

Just then his mother came in. "What have you got there?"

Mr. Kahn opened the egg and let the music play for a few moments.

"That's the waltz from *Onegin*! I love it!" Mrs. Kahn effused.

"Look at it, Ruth. Doesn't it look like a Fabergé egg?"

Mrs. Kahn took the device, shut the egg, and examined it.

Andy shared, "She said she got it at some junk shop, I think. It was filthy and had to be carefully cleaned."

"I don't know. Fabergé eggs don't grow on trees. I'm sure it's a reproduction." Mrs. Kahn put it back in its box so her husband could put it in the safe. "It is quite beautiful, though."

"Why does she want it put in a safe?" Andy's father asked.

"She just has a weird feeling that someone is going to try to steal it. She's an old lady and kind of nuts. In a nice way," Andy concluded.

Mr. Kahn said, "Well, there it is, all safe and sound in my… safe!" He pushed the metal door shut and turned the knob to make it harder to open again.

CHAPTER 14

ROBBY MET Andy at the front door of his aunt's house. "Hey, there… you ready to play detective?" Andy joked.

They had decided it was time to solve the mystery that had at first seemed like his aunt was losing her marbles but later became clear was really happening. Robby decided that when Ivy wasn't home, he and Andy should take up posts in the house, but of course they couldn't do that when school was in session. Since Ivy reported the petty thefts and returns were continuing on a regular basis, they knew the thief was still at it, though on a sinister note Ivy also reported a couple of things had never been replaced. They were apparently gone forever, so maybe they'd truly been stolen.

"Good thing we have a day for the teachers to do their paperwork. Maybe whoever is doing this won't know that, and maybe he, or she, will take a chance and come in to sneak around," Robby suggested.

They let themselves into the house. It was perfectly silent. Ivy had been gone all morning. "I hope we didn't just miss the culprit," Andy sighed.

"I know. It's such a half-baked plan, but it's the best we can do." Robby started to look around the foyer. "I wonder where we should hide?"

Andy put his forefinger to his chin. "Mmmm... where have most of the items gone missing from?

Robby answered, "The parlor or the dining room?"

The two walked into the front room that Ivy called her parlor.

"Lots of stuff in here," Andy said. He started to list the items that had gone missing. "The things on the mantel, like the coin, the old books, the set of commemorative spoons, the little Jane Austen dolls...."

Robby nodded. "And don't forget the little paintings of the cocker spaniels."

"Let's go into the dining room." Andy led the way into the overcrowded room. "With all this furniture in here, I don't know how the burglar could even get around." He walked to the big china cabinet and slid a forefinger alongside the glass in the door. "Weren't the tarot cards in here?" There were a lot of little things on all the shelves. "But it's locked, right?"

Robby came to stand next to him, gazing in at the shadowy shelves. "No, she lost the key years ago." He grabbed the cabinet handle and pulled one side of the doors open. He reached in to touch a tiny set of ornately painted teacups. "These went missing for a while, I seem to remember."

Andy shrugged. "I wish we could dust for fingerprints, but unless we had access to police records and unless our thief, or rather borrower, had a record, that wouldn't do us any good." He reached for the other door and pulled it open too. "I love these little toy soldiers." He picked one up, dressed in a uniform of some eighteenth-century European army. "Where did she get these?"

Laughing, Robby replied, "Now that would be telling!" Facing Andy's unbelieving expression, he explained, "Aunt Ivy was a teacher, right? Over the years kids would bring stuff into class, especially when she taught fifth or sixth grade, and if they were fooling around with them, she would confiscate them. She got a lot of her treasures that way."

"That was how she got that full set of the first *Star Wars* bubble gum cards, right? The ones she keeps upstairs?"

"Yeah. She told me it took her weeks to get them all, but in that case, she traded stuff for most of them. These soldiers aren't even as valuable as those cards, though. She painted them herself, but they originally came out of cereal boxes."

Andy glanced sideways at him. "How do you know all that stuff?"

He just shrugged.

The two continued to examine the dining room but decided going upstairs to Aunt Ivy's little office was the best choice for lying in wait for someone "to swipe the goods," as Robby put it.

About a half hour later, they were looking at some items on a shelf on the wall when the two boys heard a noise downstairs. Their gazes locked.

Andy's eyes were wide. "Is that...?"

"It could just be Ivy," Robby said. He listened for a few minutes. "It's not Mr. Duck. I saw him in the heated bed in Ivy's bedroom. Shh, shh!"

They looked about for some place to hide.

Andy headed for the hall closet where the linens were kept and managed to pull the door shut between himself and the hallway. Robby headed into Ivy's office, where he slipped under the guest bed.

Robby stayed as still as he could, listening for movement and not hearing much. He finally caught the sound of something hitting the floor downstairs and grimaced, wondering if they should have stayed down there.

But finally there came a squeak on the uncarpeted steps to the second level. The tread was too loud to suit Ivy's diminutive physique. This could be it!

He held his breath as he heard movement in the hall. Once it passed by, he peeked out from under the bed. He could see Andy peering out from the hall closet. He gestured for quiet and then pointed toward the bedroom door.

After a few minutes, Robby came out from under the bed very stealthily, and once in the hall, Andy joined him. They tiptoed to the open bedroom door and one on either side, they peered in.

It was Roger, Robby's uncle! He was in his usual outfit, tan slacks and a tan windbreaker over his blue cambric work shirt. He was leaning over the bed table, as if he were looking to see if anything had fallen behind it. Mr. Duck was on the bed and stared directly at the two boys in the door. But Roger didn't notice, so he didn't see the boys coming into the room.

"What are you doing, Uncle Roger?" Robby said, not hushing his voice at all.

The older man jerked up abruptly and spun around. "Oh, Robby, it's you!" He glanced at Andy, "Oh, and your friend, um, what was his name?"

"What are you doing here, Uncle Roger?" Robby asked.

Roger looked around the room. He had a cloth shopping bag around one wrist. He glanced at it, then put it behind his back. "I… I… uh… was just bringing back something of Ivy's I borrowed."

Andy reached out a hand toward the bag. "Give it to me. I'll see to it she gets it."

Roger's face went red. He shook his head. "You don't need to do that for me."

"Still," Robby said, reaching out his hand as well.

Roger stood rooted to the spot. He looked first at Robby and then Andy, then dropped his chin to his chest. He held out the bag.

Robby took it and looked inside. He reached in and pulled out an old bit of costume jewelry he remembered his Aunt Ivy kept in the jewelry box on the dresser. He held it up so Andy could look at it.

"Why, Roger, did you borrow this for some sort of dress-up party? Maybe you're into drag?" Robby smirked.

They heard the sound of the front door opening downstairs. Andy looked at Robby and nodded.

"Aunt Ivy, Robby and I are in here," he called.

When Ivy joined them, she stood staring at the trio. "My Lord!" she said. "Roger!"

Robby showed her the necklace and reached into the bag to pull out a little crystal box and some other things. "He said he borrowed them from you and was returning them."

Ivy took the necklace and stared openmouthed at Robby and then Roger. "Roger, you know that's not true. You... you stole them."

Roger glanced up at her, his face white. "You remember, don't you? I was going to have them appraised."

"*Bullshit!*" Ivy said, surprising everyone. "You stole them. Why, Roger? Why?"

SOMETIME LATER the two boys, Roger, and Ivy were in the kitchen while she brewed tea. Roger made his confession at last.

"I've... I've been having money problems," he admitted, not meeting Ivy's gaze. "I'd take a few things at a time to have them appraised. Nothing was worth much more than fifty dollars," he lamented. "I decided to wait until I had enough items to make it worth my while. I was coming back to take all the more expensive things to sell."

He shook his head, looking embarrassed. "I'm sorry, Ivy. I just figured you had so much, you would never even miss a thing."

"Roger, you could have just asked to borrow money. You know that, don't you, dear?" Ivy said, sounding sad.

Roger just stood, hanging his head.

They talked for a while longer over cups of tea. Robby noticed Roger appraising his own cup and gave the man a dirty look. He was surprised when Ivy forgave him, and he watched Roger slink out the kitchen door with his proverbial tail between his legs.

"So you aren't going to have him arrested?" Andy asked as Ivy poured more tea from the old teapot into his cup.

Robby answered for Ivy. "No, it's all in the family. He won't do it again. And we won't tell anyone."

Ivy added, "I think he learned his lesson, and since his wife took off, he's been a little, well, off." She looked at each of the boys in turn. "I can't thank you enough for uncovering his antics. I was really worried there for a while, first that there really was a burglar, and then that I was going nuts. Now I know it was really nothing."

Robby grinned at Andy, happy the mystery was finally solved.

Ivy pulled out her chair, sat, and picked up her teacup. "Well, one thing's for sure."

Robby looked up at her, waiting. "What's that, Aunt Ivy?"

Ivy grinned. "I own a lot of real junk!" All three of them broke into laughter.

ANDY FINALLY told Robby he needed to go home to get ready before it was time to drive to Olympia for the Quiz Kids competition. They bid Ivy good-bye and waited outside the door until they heard her turn the dead bolt. They got into Robby's car and headed for Andy's condo.

"I do have to ask you one thing…," Andy said nervously.

Robby glanced over at him. "What's that?'

Andy seemed a little hesitant. "Well, I was just wondering. Why weren't you afraid that the robber was someone you don't know who could be, like, dangerous?"

Robby laughed. "Now you ask me? Weren't you afraid?"

Andy looked abashed but didn't reply.

Robby responded, "I thought I told you, but maybe I didn't…. I was pretty sure it was a family member—Roger, or maybe one of the kids. I thought Roger was acting kind of suspicious. And how would anyone else know about Ivy's treasures or have a key?"

Andy let out a burst of air. "Well, I'm glad. I was caught up in it all, and I'm glad I'm all in one piece afterward."

"Me too!" Robby said firmly.

At the condo Robby promised to let Andy know when he would be coming by to pick him up.

CHAPTER 15

ROBBY PICKED up his cell phone about fifteen minutes before he would arrive at Andy's condo and punched his number. The phone rang and went to voice mail. He shut off his phone and tried a text. After five minutes he gave up. He called again and got voice mail again. He shook his head.

"Mom, Claire!" he called. "I have to go now. I have to pick up Andy."

When he got to the Kahns' condo, Andy's father answered the door. He had a newspaper in his hand and looked at Robby like he was crazy. "But you already picked Andy up!" he said.

Robby stared at him. Lamely he said, "No, I didn't."

"Well, that's odd. Ruth! Gabe!" he called to his family. When they appeared he asked, "Didn't Andy say Robby was here and he had to go?"

Gabe shrugged, but Ruth said, "Yes. He picked up his satchel of books and his coat and took off out the door."

"And there was someone outside? Did he get in their car?"

"I think so. I heard a car engine and heard the car leave. I didn't watch them," Ruth said. Her face had become strained with worry.

"Well, what could have happened? Could someone else have picked him up?" Mr. Kahn looked at Robby.

An awful feeling was growing in Robby's stomach. He remembered what Andy had said about Smartass continuing to harass him. What if he had kidnapped Andy? It was absurd, but what else could it be?

"Let me try calling him again."

He took his cell phone out of his jacket pocket and pressed Andy's number with his thumb. He held the receiver to his ear and waited. To his surprise the phone was answered. "Andy?" he said.

"No, not Andrea, you fag. We've got her, and wait until you see what we'll do to her." The call disconnected.

Robby tried to get them back on the line, but just then his phone died. "Damn, I left the charger at home." He stared at the phone in his hand, then told the Kahns, "That was Smartass, I think. Bradley Dunbar is his real name. The guy you called the cops and principal on. He and his friends have Andy."

"Oh, my little girl," Ruth said. Robby realized that in the stress of this situation, she had completely forgotten that Andy was her little boy now. She put her hand to her mouth and started crying.

Mr. Kahn announced, "Gabe, stay with your mother. Robby and I will go look for your brother."

Robby volunteered, "I'll take my car. We can cover more area that way." Mr. Kahn agreed, and they left, leaving a weeping Ruth in the house with a helpless Gabe in case Andy came home.

Andy's dad said, "Robby, I'll go look around the school, but you should go look at the parks and necking places. They might know how dark they are and take him there to scare him."

It hit Robby that he didn't know if Andy's mom was going to call the police. He decided to call home and tell his mother and Claire what was happening. He picked up his phone and started to punch numbers, but he remembered his phone was dead. "Shit!" he shouted and threw the phone on the car floor. He would have to turn around and go home to tell them.

He tore into the parking lot of the complex and didn't even try to park in a registered spot. He saw his mother and Claire coming out of the building and dashed to them.

"Smartass and his friends kidnapped Andy! I don't know where they would take him."

His mother was unable to respond in any coherent way, but Claire said, "Omigod. My phone has been missing all day. Last night Kathy Gianaris came over. Our backpacks look the same. I figured she grabbed mine. My keys and phone were in it. I was going to get them from her Monday."

"Doesn't she hang out with Grease?" Robby asked. Her sick look told him the answer was yes.

"Robby, aren't you getting carried away? How do you know that this Ass fellow took Andy?" His mother was, as usual, dismissing him.

He shouted at her, "Because the asshole told me he had him."

"Oh," his mom said. "Where would he take him?"

Robby bit his lower lip and thought fast. "I wish I had that GPS thingy on my phone so we could tell where Claire's phone is. If Kathy has it and she's with Grease and Smartass, it could show us where they have Andy."

Their mother cleared her throat. "Well, actually, I have that. I have both your phones on it so I know where you are." She looked like she was prepared to be screamed at or hit.

Instead both Robby and Claire grabbed her and kissed her. "Thank God!" Robby said.

He snatched his mother's phone from her hand as she drew it out of her purse.

"Call my phone," Claire commanded.

He punched the buttons for Claire's number, but halfway through his mother said, "Just do star-02."

He looked at his mother and asked, both sarcastically and somewhat hopefully, "I suppose I'm star-01?"

"No, that's 9-1-1," she replied.

"I should've guessed," he said. He hit star-02. The phone on the other end rang several times, then was answered. "Yeah, whaddya want?"

"What does it say?" Claire was bouncing on her toes.

"Let me see," he said. Robby looked at the tiny screen and chose the app for the GPS. It showed a small map. He looked at it, trying to identify the location. Just as the person on the other end hung up, he saw what he needed to know. "The high school! Or somewhere near it."

Claire ran to the car and got into the driver's seat. The keys were still in the ignition. "Let's go!"

"But I have to call Ivy. She's expecting us to come pick her up to take her to Olympia. And shouldn't we call the police first?" their mother asked, her voice shaking with nerves. "I tell you what. I'll stay here and call from our home phone. You go, and the police will meet you there." She turned and headed for the apartment vestibule.

Robby hopped into the car, still holding his mother's cell phone. Claire had already stepped on the gas, and he almost didn't make it into the seat. He pulled the door closed as the car sped away.

At the high school, Claire drove into the parking lot and parked haphazardly in the principal's spot. She leaped out of the car. "Where should we look?"

Robby had no idea. He got out of the car and glanced around. "I guess we should just check around the outside. The school is locked. They can't have gotten in."

Claire ran to the building and tried the door anyway. "Nope, you're right. Let's go to the sports field."

As she and Robby came around the building and into the space behind it, they could see a small group of students walking away from one end of the football field. "There they are!" Claire called.

It was too late for Smartass and his friends to scatter. Or maybe they just wanted a confrontation. Robby saw the tallest of the kids hanging back, while the others were urging him to leave with them. As he approached he saw, as he suspected, that the tall kid was Bradley Dunbar himself. And there, not far from Bradley, was another figure. Robby's heart almost stopped. It was Andy! He was tied to the single vertical part of the goalpost, and he was completely naked.

The other kids with Smartass hung back, seemingly not wanting to leave but not wanting to get caught. Robby heard his sister spit, "Kathy! You bitch!" He thought he recognized the girl who was running back in the direction of the school building.

"Smartass, let's go!" said the boy known as Smack.

"It's too late for that now," Robby said. "I see you and Grease too, and one of the girls."

"That's Sophie DeNardo," Claire informed him.

"No, it's not," said Smartass. "It's your pretty little girlfriend, Andrea. Can you see it? She's got a pussy!"

Robby raced to Andy and tried to see how to untie him. As Bradley claimed, Andy had a girl's genitals, and without the binder, his breasts showed. He took off his jacket and tried to cover Andy from the waist down.

"Just get me untied, you jerk," Andy said.

"I'm trying," Robby said, struggling with the knots in the plasticized rope Smartass had used. He managed to get one of the knots loose.

Claire was screaming at the boys and Sophie. "You pigs! How could you do a thing like this? Don't you know this is a crime? A felony? It's kidnapping, and you can go to prison for that."

Smartass sneered, "Andy's a freak. And my dad is a lawyer. We'll get a slap on the wrist."

"I'm eighteen," called Smack. "And you are too now, Smartass."

"Me too," said Grease. "I'd be tried as an adult."

As he struggled with another knot, Andy squirming to untie the same one, Robby said, "You all are."

"Call my mom and dad," begged Andy.

"My phone is dead."

"But Mom's isn't. What's your number?" Claire had their mother's phone in her hand.

Andy gave their home phone number, and Claire called it. They could hear her hurriedly speaking into the phone.

By the time the knot came loose, all the kids but Smartass had run away. Andy shook his arms to knock the ropes off. "Where are my clothes?"

Bradley raised one arm and shook the wad of clothing he had in that hand. "I have them."

Andy roared and charged him. He stepped away, but Andy changed course and knocked him to the ground. In an instant Andy was on him, punching him in the face.

"Just sit on him," Robby screamed.

Andy kept punching Smartass over and over until Robby grabbed his arms and made him stop. He could hear Andy weeping with anger.

Smartass lay on the ground with his lip and nose bleeding. "You freak," he swore at Andy.

Claire had taken off after the others and was dragging Sophie back by the arm of her jacket.

Robby was on his knees, his arms around Andy from the back. He was trying to calm him. Andy finally subsided when Robby heard running feet and looked in that direction. He couldn't tell who it was at first, but he heard what sounded like police radios. Sure enough, one and then another cop ran up. One grabbed Andy off Smartass and started to handcuff him. "No, wait, he's not the bad guy," Robby shouted.

The cop seemed to notice then that the girl he was grappling with was naked. He looked at Robby and asked, "He?"

"Give me my pants," Andy demanded.

Robby riffled around in the confusion of clothing Smartass had dropped and found a pair of slacks. He handed them to Andy, who the cop had let go, and put the pants on with no underwear.

Andy demanded, "My shirt! I'm cold."

The cop had Smartass on his feet and handcuffed. The other cop had ahold of Sophie and Claire. Claire was screaming and swearing at him.

"That's my sister. She's okay," Robby said.

"Which one?" the cop asked.

"The one who's swearing," said Andy.

The cop let go of Claire and Sophie but glared at them. "Don't move until we get this all sorted out," he warned the two girls.

They heard running feet again. This time it was Mr. Kahn. He ran to Andy crying, "Andy! What did they do to you?" Andy had his shirt and pants on by now.

"They kidnapped him, stripped him, and tied him to the goalpost," Robby informed Mr. Kahn and the cops. The police officer who had handcuffed Smartass took out a notebook and started asking questions.

Looking at Smartass, the cop said, "What happened?"

After identifying himself to the officer as Bradley Dunbar, Smartass said, "I have no idea what they're talking about. I was just walking by the high school when these lunatics ran up and attacked me."

The cop raised his head from his notebook and asked, "Then why was this one naked?"

Bradley shrugged. "He, um, she was making out with her boyfriend there."

The cop looked at Robby, clearly confused.

Claire stomped her foot. "That's my brother, Robby, and he was not making out with anyone. We got here and found Andy tied to the goalpost. Smartass there was responsible. Him and his friends. One of them had my cell phone, and that's how

131

we found them. You asshole!" she screamed and attacked the handcuffed Bradley.

"Whoa, whoa," said the cop who stood nearest them, grabbing her by the shoulders and pulling her off Bradley.

Mr. Kahn was holding Andy but looked at Bradley. "How could you do such a thing? What kind of a person are you?"

The boy just made inarticulate noises of denial.

Mr. Kahn started to guide Andy away from the scene. "Hey, wait a minute. We saw this kid attacking this guy. We have to arrest him," the cop said.

Mr. Kahn looked confused. "But he was the one who was kidnapped. And he needs medical attention. They may have raped him."

"We'll take him to the hospital in custody," the other officer said.

Mr. Kahn looked flustered. Then he said firmly, "I'll drive him to the hospital, and you can escort us."

"Oh, Dad," Andy protested. "I'm fine. I'm just really pissed off."

Everyone was startled when Mr. Kahn snapped, "Shut up, Andy. Do as you're told."

Andy was speechless.

The lead cop broke in. "I have to insist, sir. She's a victim of a crime and we have to take her to the emergency room."

Mr. Kahn snapped, "Him!" making the cops look confused and Andy smile. "All right, then. Andy, I'll call your mother too." Taking out his cell phone, Mr. Kahn called home to talk to Ruth.

Robby and Claire both put their hands on Andy's shoulders. "It'll be all right. We'll meet you at the hospital. Evergreen?"

At the officer's nod, Robby gave Andy a peck on the cheek. Then he and Claire turned to where they had left the car.

TWO HOURS later Robby and Claire found themselves in the waiting room of Emergency Services at Evergreen again. Their mother had arrived only minutes before. When they thanked her for calling the police, she said "Sure" weakly and walked off to get a cup of coffee from a vending machine.

"Really worried, wasn't she?" Claire exclaimed to her brother. "And where is Aunt Ivy?"

All Robby could do was shrug.

Mr. and Mrs. Kahn and Gabe were all in an examination room with Andy. After a short time, one of the cops came out and talked to the Czerwinskis. Robby and Claire between them described the events of the evening. The officer wrote it all down.

"What's going to happen?" Robby asked.

The officer looked up from his notebook. "To her or to the boy who did this?"

Robby said irritably, "Him." He realized that by "him," the officer would think he meant Bradley and explained, "To the boy in the emergency room."

"Oh, you mean the girl, I mean the transgender boy?" The cop was older and seemed to be still taking it all in. "I can't tell you. Privacy rules and all. But we're not charging her, um, him, and I don't think he will press charges."

Robby almost shouted. "The boy who did this! What about arresting *him*?"

The police officer said, "Calm down. We have him and the girl in custody. We're looking for the other two boys and the other girl. When we find them all, we'll decide what to charge them with, if anything."

"If *anything*?" Claire screeched.

At a sound from the emergency room door, they all looked up to see Mr. and Mrs. Kahn and Andy coming out. Robby and Claire called "Andy" and jumped up and dashed to him.

"Don't make a fuss," Andy said in a low tone, while his parents checked him out at the reception desk. "You are such a drama queen."

Ignoring Andy's comment, Robby asked him, "But why are you out here?"

Andy gestured to some seats by Gabe, and they all went to sit. "I'm perfectly all right. Just shaken up and some cuts and bruises. I would rather just go home."

Robby shook his head. "But the trauma!"

Andy rolled his eyes. "I just want to go home." After a short pause, he said, "I wonder what happened at the Quiz Kid tournament?"

THE NEXT morning Robby called Andy with what he had learned about the tournament. "It's kind of funny, really. We had alternates, so when we didn't show up, they just put two in our places. But then they found out that Walla Walla Full Gospel High had had a wild party the night before at one of the area motels and gotten busted. They were disqualified from the Quiz Kid completion. So Highlands View won."

"No," Andy said. "You aren't serious."

"I certainly am. But how are you this morning?"

Andy said, "I'm all right. I'm just waiting to hear what will happen to the kids who attacked me."

"They wouldn't tell us anything about that. Will you be at school tomorrow?" Robby asked.

"I think I need a week off." It was the first time Andy had shown any indication that the experience of the past evening was anything more than a walk in the park.

Andy continued, "I gotta get over all the humiliating things they had to check. Like... the pelvic exam."

Robby didn't understand at first, but then it hit him. "Were you raped?" he asked in horror.

"No," Andy replied with a note of *How stupid are you?* in his voice. "And they could tell that right away."

Robby said, "I don't understand...," but then he realized he should drop it. "Never mind," he said, embarrassed.

"Good. Can I come over and see you?"

"Of course you can."

CHAPTER 16

MONDAY MORNING at school without Andy was lonely, but Robby made his way to biology class, dragging his feet.

"Hey, dude" came a familiar voice in the hallway.

Robby looked up to find Max sprinting up to him. "Oh, hey, Max. I got to get to biology."

Max put a hand on Robby's arm. "I heard about Saturday and what happened to Andy. It's all over school." He was looking into Robby's face with worry and compassion.

"Yeah," Robby said. "Andy's shaken up but okay. Did you hear about the Quiz Kids?"

The grin crossing Max's handsome face showed he most certainly had.

"Pretty funny, huh? But I would rather we had won the tournament outright." Robby shrugged.

"I know. Well, you get on to class. Hey, did you get the announcement about graduation?"

"My God! That's in just a few weeks, right?" It struck Robby, whose mind had been full of recent events. "I guess we're going to get our gowns and stuff soon."

Robby started to walk away, but he turned and called to the retreating Max, "Hey, you still going to WSU?"

"Yeah, of course. And you know what?" He gave Robby a shy but happy grin.

"What?"

"I looked it up. They have a GLBT center and activities." His smile was pure pleasure.

Robby flashed him a grin. "All right!" Robby called and nodded. "It starts, huh?"

Max nodded sharply. "It already has, my friend. It already has." His shit-eating grin said it all.

Robby went into the classroom and sat down on his usual stool, giving Andy's empty one a wistful look.

Mrs. Pollack called the class to order. "We have a guest speaker this morning." Robby looked at the young woman who sat, dressed in a simple linen suit with her hair in a neat bun, in a chair at the front of the class.

Mrs. Pollack introduced her as Josephine Eng. She explained that as they were in the section of the curriculum to talk about the range of sexual preferences, they were starting at one end of the continuum. She said that Ms. Eng represented an organization called the "Asexual Visibility and Awareness Network or AVEN." She turned the floor over to the young woman, who stood and started to address the class.

As she spoke about the facts about asexuality, Robby's eyes grew wider and wider. As Ms. Eng explained, "Asexuality does not mean a lack of interest in sex at all, but only that the individual does not find either men or women sexually attractive. Unlike celibacy, which is a choice, asexuality is a sexual orientation. Asexual people have the same emotional needs as everybody else and are just as capable of forming intimate relationships."

She went on to say, "As humans, we are in general a social species, programmed to support each other in family units and communities, and it seems often mob rule dictates what is normal, expected, or acceptable behavior. Especially in a modern society where the media projects these ideas into every facet of our lives, we are now educated very early on as to how life apparently is. No matter what our true feelings inside, we may now attempt to adhere to the 'rules' that we have collectively set ourselves."

Robby thought about what she said. He knew full well how society pressured gay and lesbian people to be "straight," and he had a new awareness of how it demanded a person identify as either a boy or a girl depending on certain external factors. Andy had taught him that one's brain should determine what gender one is. But why did everyone think that whatever gender identity or sexual preference a person had, they had to have *some* preference? Why couldn't someone find his or her place sexually other than on one end of the continuum or another? He or she could be either fully straight or fully gay or lesbian, or he or she could be asexual!

He listened raptly as Ms. Eng went on, finding something familiar in every word. "I've long grown used to the idea of asexuality, and I know it fits me better than any other orientation. I know that I've never experienced sexual attraction. I do have a libido, and I find it a rather pointless part of my being. If I lost it—apart from the worry of a medical issue if it went!—I wouldn't miss it. I am 'out' on all my frequent websites online and to my brother and cousin, but not to my parents because I know they wouldn't accept it. It's a lot easier to be 'out' online, but I did go to Pride London 2010 in order to help raise visibility, even though social situations and one-to-one visibility makes me very uncomfortable. I am one of those people to whom asexuality is just a part of who I am, not something I need to shout about for my own sake. I shout about it for the sake of others. I'm glad at least that I was stubborn in school. I'm glad that I'm not that romantically inclined, so I'm not in the desperate situation of trying to make a mixed-orientation relationship work. I'm glad that I got to know myself before having or trying to share myself with a life partner. If I had tried to have a girlfriend or, when same-sex marriage was made legal, a wife, I may have had the grim experience of cheating someone out of a complete relationship. At least complete in the traditional sense."

It felt like rockets were going off in Robby's brain. He knew things might change for him, but this all sounded exactly right. It wasn't that he was underdeveloped. He was just who he was. If Andy, who he knew he loved, didn't want a sexless relationship, they would go their separate ways, or they would find a compromise. But he wondered if it was possible they could have the sort of partnership that some asexual people had.

Mrs. Pollack opened the floor for the class to ask questions.

"Have you ever had sex?" asked one girl.

"I haven't, but any number of asexual people have. Sometimes the desire coincides with an act. But with someone who is asexual, that is not necessarily what follows. Let me give you an example. Let's say you smell coffee and think, 'That smells good.' That's attraction. If you decide then that you want coffee, that's desire. But you can smell and like the smell of coffee but not want any, and you can want coffee without smelling it first. I know this sounds confusing, but that's how it is for me. I'd rather have a girlfriend I can cuddle with than go to her for an orgasm. But I can have an orgasm on my own."

The giggles and titters irritated Robby, who wanted to hear what Ms. Eng said without the distraction.

"But won't you just grow out of it?" a boy asked.

"I might," Ms. Eng said, "or I might not. I don't think I will, given that I'm well into my twenties now, but if it happens, it happens."

One timid girl was so quiet that Ms. Eng had to ask her to speak up. She said, "It sounds like you're describing just being human. I mean, I'm not always into… um… sex, but sometimes I might be."

Ms. Eng nodded. "The point is that you get to decide. Scientifically we know there is a continuum, but we can't scientifically insist you be on any one point in it. That's up to you at any given time."

"This is bullshit," said one boy irritably. "You're just frigid and want to make up a reason."

Robby looked at Mrs. Pollack to see if she would call the boy on his comment, but she just smiled thinly and let Ms. Eng respond. "You can say that, but you don't really know, do you?"

Another boy asked, "Can you just have sexual attraction if you are in a loving relationship but not otherwise?"

Nodding, Ms. Eng said, "That might be called 'demisexual' or 'gray asexual.' Again, the point is that you get to decide who and what you are."

A girl sitting in the front row commented, "That sounds so lonely and sad. Don't you want a husband and kids?"

"I don't," said Ms. Eng. "But I know other asexual people who do. My friend Adam, for instance. He has a wife. They have two kids. They have a pretty typical marriage. They've been together for about twelve years. Like most married couples, sex has become less important for them. The only difference is that it never was for Adam. They've had their family and their partnership. That's what matters. If you look at statistics, some married couples stop having sex at some point anyway, and that seems to be as true or truer for gay or lesbian couples. It's not that strong a drive for a lot of people."

"Now that *is* depressing" came a boy's voice from the third row.

Ms. Eng said, "Only if you have other expectations. Some people find it rather comforting. Our society and the media preaches sex, sex, sex. There's a lot more to life than that."

Robby couldn't wait anymore. "If a person never feels sexual attraction for anyone ever, isn't the choice being taken out of their hands?"

With a knowing smile, Ms. Eng replied, "It might, or it might not. A person might find that to be the case, but it just isn't up to anyone else."

Robby found himself thinking that what Ms. Eng was talking about was just a logical construct. If he accepted the concept of a continuum of sexuality, he would have to accept a starting point. That's all it was, an idea. But then he thought about his own experience, which he had to admit tended to bear it all out.

When Ms. Eng finished answering she reached for a stack of brochures and passed them out. They were from AVEN and its website. She said, "It has a FAQ which you can find at http://www.asexuality.org."

Robby couldn't wait to talk this over with Andy, though at the same time he was terrified of how Andy would respond. He had trouble paying attention in his next classes and skipped lunch to call Andy. When he didn't answer, Robby sent him a text, saying that in biology class they talked about something he needed to talk to him about.

THAT AFTERNOON Andy answered his knock at the condo door.

"Wow, you are hyped up. What's this all about?"

Robby asked, "Can we talk in your room?" When they got there, he closed and locked the door. He stood with his back to it, his hands in front of him, fidgeting. "I don't know where to start, and I'm terrified what you will say. Let me start by just saying that I know I love you, that I'm in love with you. You make my heart sing, and I want to spend the rest of my life with you. If you don't feel the same way, well, that will be awful, but you have to do what's right for you."

Andy sat on his bed, his mouth open in shock.

"Maybe I should just tell you all about what we talked about in biology today."

Andy nodded and sat with his hands folded in his lap, listening patiently.

Robby told him about Ms. Eng and AVEN. He explained, "Ms. Eng said she couldn't speak for anyone else, but she knew she at least so far had no sexual feelings about anyone. She said there were people who sometimes had sexual relationships. It's not all black and white." He went on to say that asexuality and celibacy were not the same thing, that celibacy was a choice and asexuality was just who you are.

As Robby talked, he kept a close eye on Andy's face. He seemed to be listening to it all, occasionally nodding or making a "*hmm*" sound.

"What do you think?" Robby finally said. He waited, tense.

Andy gestured for him to sit by him on his bed.

"That's a lot of information," Andy began. "So you believe you might be asexual. That could change, but it might not. And you want to be in a relationship with me, but we would just kiss and cuddle. Right?"

"I'm not really sure. I might sometimes want to make love to you. In fact, I'm pretty sure I will. But it would be more romantic, loving, than sexy. Would that be enough for you?" Robby asked anxiously.

Andy was sitting on the bed with his legs bent and crossed at the ankles. He leaned forward to put his elbows on his knees and his chin in his hands. "Hmm. Let me think."

Robby waited, tense with anticipation.

Andy finally spoke. "I honestly don't know. I love you, Robby, very much. The idea of living with you and even marrying you appeals to me strongly. I suppose if I were to get aroused, I could masturbate, right?"

"Well, sure, and me too."

"And sometimes we might do it together?"

"I don't see why not," Robby said, starting to feel hopeful.

"You know I might never get myself a cock, right?"

Robby nodded.

"So I might always have nothing but a vagina. Do you think you would ever want to... well... fuck me?"

Robby shrugged. "Would you want to be fucked?" he asked.

They looked at each other. Robby felt the corner of his mouth start to go up. In no time he was laughing, and Andy was too.

"I love this," Andy said. "I love how we can talk and laugh together. I don't think too many people have that, that sort of cuddly buddy stuff."

Robby reached for Andy and took him in his arms. "I love *you*. That's all I know."

EPILOGUE

ROBBY AND Andy graduated valedictorian and salutatorian in their class. It doesn't matter which was which. They were both accepted at the University of Washington. They knew that school had a GLBT center and decided to join it. They wanted to share a dormitory room and reserved one together.

Bradley Dunbar and his cronies were arrested for kidnapping and sexual assault, not to mention trespassing on school grounds with the intention of committing felonies, but Bradley fled the jurisdiction. The last they heard of him was that he was somewhere in South America where he could not be extradited. The other two boys were tried as adults. They got brief sentences in prison, and the girls received community service. The Kahns, with Andy's reluctant consent, filed restraining orders against them, though the girls made no attempt to violate it. But a civil suit against all the families wound up with a settlement that pretty much paid for Andy's college. All of the criminals, as they were now known, were expelled from school, denied participation in graduation, had to attend a special bullying program the school arranged, and take their entire senior year again before they were given their diplomas.

Aunt Ivy was like some sort of avenging angel. She fussed over Andy endlessly, to his complete embarrassment. She got involved in an antibullying society herself and dragged Robby along, Andy refusing to go. She was vociferous about all the historical figures she knew of who had been persecuted: the Japanese Americans in World War II, the Stonewall Riots, the Cuban expulsion of all their gay people, lynchings in the South, you name it. "At least Castro admitted he had been wrong when he said gay people were 'agents of imperialism'!" She punctuated her outrage with a succinct "As if!"

Antiques Roadshow was quite the experience. Besides Aunt Ivy and Robby and Andy, the Khans and Gabe also went to the taping. At first they just stood in line, waiting to get their registration verified. Then they stood in line with Aunt Ivy, cradling the box with the egg in her arms, and waited to talk to an appraiser. The woman who came out to look at the egg held it for a few minutes, then quickly excused herself. They waited some more.

Finally two people, a man in a suit and a woman with a laptop, came and asked Aunt Ivy to come with them. Aunt Ivy insisted Robby and Andy be allowed to come with her. They went into a small room and stood while the man took the box and opened it. He carefully removed the egg and stood gaping at it. He exchanged looks with the woman.

"This might be something quite extraordinary," he said. "Or it might be a reproduction."

Ivy nodded and smiled. "We know that."

Over the next hour, several people came into the room and looked at the music box. The woman went to the computer and looked at several websites with eggs pictured on them. The people left the room, Ivy and the boys waiting for them to come back, and finally the man in the suit asked them to come with him.

They found themselves at a table with a camera and cameraman standing behind it. People kept glancing their way, but the stagehands kept them at bay. Finally the camera lights went on, and Ivy stood with the man in the suit looking at the music box as the man began to speak.

"You say you got this music box in a junk shop?"

Aunt Ivy just nodded but when prompted, she spoke aloud, "Yes, I did. It was really a mess. I had to get it cleaned up and oiled before we could open it and listen to the tune."

The man nodded impatiently. "You had it cleaned by a jeweler?"

"No, my neighbor who fixes cars did it."

The look on the man's face bordered on horror. "I see."

He picked up the music box and carefully flipped the latch. The spring in the latch made the top of the red enamel egg with the gold accents pop open. The stage director gestured for the cameraman to zoom in on the egg. The little ballerina began to twirl with the bell-like sound of the *Onegin* waltz starting right at the beginning. Robby realized the stage director must have made sure when the egg opened that the music was at the first bars of the waltz.

The man in the suit started to speak again. "This music box at first appeared to be a Fabergé egg, called Imperial Eggs in the czar's court. We looked into its history and discovered that the creator, Peter Carl Fabergé, made more than fifty of these eggs. They are all fine jeweler's art. After the Russian Revolution, Vladimir Lenin had them all collected from the palace, the private houses where they were kept, and also the ones still at the jewelers. In the 1930s Stalin put the collection together and sold them to Armand Hammer, the American industrialist who was a friend of Vladimir Lenin. Several appeared to have been lost, maybe destroyed to sell the gold and jewels for the Politburo."

"This one was lost for many, many years. It was photographed in the 1890s, having been made in 1889 by Fabergé. It is called the Imperial Czarina Egg and disappeared during the time after the Revolution. We don't know what happened to it, or how it got into the hands of the owner of the junk shop. But it definitely is one of the original Imperial Eggs." He gestured to the stage director, who told the cameraman, also in gestures, to put up a still of the egg. Robby and Andy didn't know this until they saw the episode later.

The man went on to explain that the waltz from the opera *Yevgeny* or *Eugene Onegin* was playing on the music box. He told the audience about Piotr Ilych Tchaikovsky and the opera written in 1879.

"Now I understand that it used to have a tiny key to wind it up?"

Ivy assured him it had. She explained that no one could find the key, but they had found a way to set the music.

"That is too bad," said the man in the suit. "If the egg had been complete, it would have been worth more than thirty million dollars."

Ivy's jaw dropped. "W-what is it worth without the key?"

The man in the suit asked her, "What do you think it's worth?"

She looked at him, dazed. "I don't know, maybe a few hundred thousand?"

He grinned. "At least ten million dollars at auction."

"Ka-ching!" Robby and Andy chorused, dancing around and hugging each other and Ivy.

"What will you do with it?" the man asked Ivy.

She looked at the egg and laughed and said, "Nothing. I'll keep it."

The look on the man's face showed he thought she might be a lunatic, but he was off camera at the time.

Aunt Ivy did keep the egg. She had a Lucite box made for it and mounted it on a shelf on the wall of her office. She paid to have an electronic security system put in at her house. She constantly let it go unarmed, however. When she died several years later, though, it was still in her possession, and in her will she left it to her nephew Robby and his husband Andy. The two of them donated the egg to the National Gallery in Washington, DC.

THAT FALL after they learned the truth about Aunt Ivy's egg on *Antiques Roadshow*, Robby and Andy started school at the University of Washington.

The first night in their shared dorm room, Robby pushed the two beds together. Andy climbed into bed with him. They put their arms around each other, and Robby rested his head on Andy's shoulder, with a sigh of contentment.

"I love you, Robby," Andy said.

"I love you, Andy."

Robby felt complete, with Andy in his arms and sure that he wanted the same things Robby did. The sigh that left his lips said it all.

AUTHOR'S NOTES

YOU CAN find out more about asexuality at Asexuality Visibility and Awareness Network at http://www.asexuality.org.

There is a great deal online about being transgender. Gender Odyssey, http://www.genderodyssey.org, is a great resource. Any search on the terms transgender, trans woman, trans man, FTM, and MTF, as well as genderqueer, should lead you to a great many resources and groups. Also for those who are trans men, there is the fabulous site called Hudson's FTM Resource Guide at http://www.ftmguide.org/, a sort of step by step, "one stop shopping" site about everything from surgery to clothing to "packers." Finally you can't go wrong by taking a look at Transgress Press at http://www.transgresspress.com, with books on all sorts of aspects of being transgender.

There is also information about asexuality at the Matthew Shepard Foundation at http://www.matthewshepard.org/asexuality, a site with information on hate crimes against gay, lesbian, bisexual, and transgender people too. Learn all you can about how teenagers and adults can fight the senseless violence against people who just don't match the mainstream. Also see the book *Hate Crimes: Causes, Controls, and Controversies* by Phyllis B. Gerstenfeld http://www.amazon.com/Hate-Crimes-Causes-Controls-Controversies-ebook/dp/00LXFGBBS/.

I had quite a time finding a name for the scholastic competition that I finally called "Quiz Kids". There is a games company called WizKids, but at least that isn't a competition. The earlier choices I tried, Mathletics, turned out to be something quite different, and both Academia and Academica were in use. I based the competition on High School Bowl which was based on GE College Bowl which ran on CBS and NBC for many years. There are High School Bowl competitions in local high school television markets even now.

Could Ivy have found a Faberge egg? An article at CNN. com from March 20, 2014, concerned a Midwestern man who owned a small Faberge egg that he hoped to have melted down and get $500 for the gold. As it happened, he discovered an article by looking for "egg" and the name on the egg, "Vacheron Constantin," online. His search brought up a 2011 article in Britain's Daily Telegraph newspaper describing a "frantic search" for the object: the Third Imperial Easter Egg, made by Fabergé for the Russian royal family and estimated to be worth 20 million pounds ($33 million).

However, the Imperial Czarina Egg is my invention, created to allow for the fantasy we all have to find a priceless *objet d'art*.

The author welcomes any questions about any of this and will discuss the book if you write to him, Christopher Hawthorne Moss, at christopherhmoss@gmail.com. You can find out about his books at his web site, http://www.authorchristophermoss.blogspot. com and on Facebook at http://www.facebook.com/kitmoss2012.

CHRISTOPHER HAWTHORNE MOSS has dedicated his writing and Internet resource development career to fostering a history and a heritage for GLBTQ people everywhere. As he is fond of saying, "We were here, and we were queer!" As a transgender man, he is also gay and therefore has a particular interest in helping gender-variant people feel included in a culture of positivity. His belief is that plausible stories of GLBTQ people will do more good for inclusion than any other effort.

Kit lives with his husband and their two doted-upon cats in the beautiful Pacific Northwest. He has the glorious distinction of being one of three siblings, all of whom are gender variant.

He writes for both Dreamspinner Press and Harmony Ink Press.

Website: www.writerchristophermoss.com
E-mail: christopherhmoss@gmail.com

BELOVED PILGRIM

CHRISTOPHER HAWTHORNE MOSS

At the time of the earliest Crusades, young noblewoman Elisabeth longs to be the person she's always known is hidden inside. When her twin brother perishes from a fever, Elisabeth takes his identity to live as a man, a knight. As Elias, he travels to the Holy Land, to adventure, passion, death, and a lesson that honor is sometimes found in unexpected places.

Elias must pass among knights and soldiers, survive furious battle, deadly privations, moral uncertainty, and treachery if he'll have any chance of returning to his newfound love in the magnificent city of Constantinople.

CHAPTER ONE
GOD WILLS IT

WITH A loud crack, the sword came down on a helm already knocked askew by an earlier blow. The helm flew off and the wearer staggered and nearly lost his feet.

"Ho, valiantly done!" fifteen-year-old Elisabeth von Winterkirche called from her perch on the wooden fence.

Her twin brother Elias made a mock bow. "I thank you, my lady."

"You always take his side," said the other boy, Albrecht, who like Elias was squire to Sigismund von Winterkirche, the twins' father.

"He's a better fighter than you are," she stated emphatically.

"And better looking too," Elias quipped. He preened, stroking the barest shadow of beard growing on his chin.

"I will concede that point," the shorter, darker boy said. Elias looked at him with that funny, knowing smile that irritated his sister so. It just did not seem to fit.

Albrecht leaned to pick up his helm and put it back on his head. "If this damned thing had straps, it wouldn't come off so easily."

Elias let out a bark of derisive laughter. "Oh, is that why I keep knocking it off? It's not my mighty and well-delivered blows. It's the lack of straps." He lifted his chin and waved his fingers at his own throat. "Look, no straps here either. But my helm is sitting securely on my head."

Albrecht muttered something that made Elisabeth burst out laughing.

"What did he say?" her brother demanded.

"He said your swelled head fills it so much it is stuck," she explained.

Elias took a stance with his wooden sword tilted up from his right side. "Have at me, varlet. I shall not brook such ignoble insults!"

The two hefted their small shields and began to move in a counterclockwise circle, each looking for openings in the other boy's defenses. Elisabeth, unlike most girls, did not watch the practice fighting for her own entertainment. She watched each move while imagining herself in combat, detecting as best she could what each opponent was trying to do, what might work better, and what she would try given the chance. Those chances did come, for the twins had been each other's only companion through their father's absences and mother's frequent illnesses. Only when Albrecht came to serve at Winterkirche did Elias have anyone else to practice fighting with him. Elisabeth itched to get in on this fight but contented herself for now just critiquing the boys' moves.

Each had his practice sword up and held parallel to the upper edge of his shield. She had long known a fighter had to keep his sword up above the level of his opponent's shield if he had any hope of landing a blow to the body. Striking the heavy wooden shield was not without its utility, if one could deliver a hard enough blow to knock the shield askew. Elias and Albrecht knew each other's skills well enough not to waste effort on this move. They circled each other looking for a head shot.

Elias, the taller, repeatedly brought his sword swinging around to strike Albrecht's shoulder or head, but Albrecht managed over and over to raise his shield enough to block the blow or to meet sword with sword, resulting in the sharp thwack of wooden blades. Elias constantly pressed forward, making Albrecht retreat. Elisabeth pressed her lips tightly together with impatience. Elias's greatest flaw was that he was all forward motion, aggression, and not enough defense. If only Albrecht would use that against him. Elias got in some bruising blows on the shorter boy's right arm. Elisabeth mentally registered the point, but the fighters did not pause.

"Oh, for God's sake," she finally cried, jumping down from the fence. "This is getting tedious. Let me fight him."

The boys stopped and stared at her. "Fight whom?" her brother asked.

"You, Elias. Albrecht just lets you chase him around the yard. Give me your weapon."

Albrecht looked at Elias.

"Go ahead. She won't break anything," Elias said, rolling his eyes.

Elisabeth let Albrecht slip the shield onto her right arm, his helm on her head, and finally hand her the wooden sword.

The siblings took their fighting stances. Elisabeth let Elias come forward, backing up as he fully expected she would. When he seemed to put all his force into the motion, she stopped retreating and came at him, raining blows everyplace she could. He was startled at first but regained his stability, then hauled off and gave her a bruising whack on the hip. She dropped to her knees but did not concede.

Elias grinned at her. He widened his stance and took a step forward. She lifted her sword as if to swing around and catch him right of his sword, where one elbow had appeared. He laughed and moved so his shield was up and between them. She let her sword go back around and come up from below. His unprotected groin received all the might she could muster.

He staggered back, his mouth wide open but no sound issuing forth. Collapsing to his knees, he dropped his sword and shield. He put his leather-gauntleted hands to his groin and toppled over sideways.

Elisabeth lifted her arms and crowed with triumph. She danced around in place, chanting, "Yes, yes, yes!" When she looked around again, she saw Albrecht kneeling by her brother, his arms out at his sides, at a loss for how to help him.

"He'll live to suffer worse blows than that" came a deep male voice from behind her. She turned to look at Elias's and Albrecht's sword master, Dagobert. "Just let him lie there a bit and give him small sips of this." He handed a waterskin to Albrecht, then turned to Elisabeth. "Madam, you take advantage of how much he underestimates you. If you were not his sister, he would decimate you."

She scowled at him.

"And you put me in a difficult position. Your mother has begged me to discourage your interest in fighting." He looked to where Albrecht was helping Elias sit up. "Speaking of your mother, she wants you both. She has had a messenger."

The twins found Adalberta in her solar. She sat in a window embrasure with her embroidery in her lap, her eyes closed and her head back against the frame of the window. She looked as drained as ever. For all her protests that she was feeling stronger, neither of her children could ever see evidence of it. When she heard them come in, she opened her eyes, straightened, and tried to make it look like she had been busily stitching. As little interest as Elisabeth had in such things, she could see there had been no progress on the altar cloth in at least two days.

"My darlings, I have the happiest of news! I have had word from your father. The Lombards have let the imperial party cross their land. The four-year exile is over!"

The joyful look on their mother's face was not feigned. The two young people hurried forward to kneel at her feet. "Oh, Mother, at long last!"

"I know it has been very hard on you, my dears, to be without your father. And Elias, I know you have taken it hard not to have the chance to leave home to squire in another household. I will never stop being grateful that you agreed to stay here with me, especially at first when I was so ill."

The twins managed to hide the shared knowledge that their mother had never in their memory been anything but ill. "Is Father coming home soon?" Elias asked.

"He must go with the emperor's army to Cologne; then he and his household knights and men will come south to us. In a few days, maybe more. But after all this time, I think we can wait patiently."

Elisabeth pressed one of her mother's hands against her cheek. "Oh no, we can't." She laughed.

ELISABETH CURSED like one of the grooms as she tugged the hem of her skirt from the bramble where it was caught. "Damn, if I could just wear britches like Elias and Albrecht, I shouldn't have to deal with skirts!"

It was her constant refrain of late: "I wish I was a boy." Boys could learn to use weapons, boys could climb trees, boys could go off for hours and wander in the countryside, and boys did not have to sit still in Mother's solar and learn excruciatingly dull needlework.

She knew Elias and Albrecht were not far. They had given her the slip earlier that afternoon and gone off with their bows to their favorite patch of woods. Elisabeth was becoming weary of this phase in Elias's life. For months she had found her brother spending more and more time with his friend and leaving her behind. Her mother told her it was natural, and that soon she would be more interested in ladies' concerns, as her brother was in men's. "Balls," she muttered under her breath, delighted at her own audacity.

Serve him right if he misses Father's homecoming. He knew Father's party was expected today. Where is he? she wondered as she pushed her way through the scrub.

As she rounded the edge of a small coppice of trees, she thought she saw movement. There they are! She slowed her progress, wanting to surprise her brother and his friend.

She heard a yelp, which meant that whomever was chasing had caught the other. Probably it was Elias, the taller and older, by a year, of Father's two squires. She stepped forward to make herself known and froze.

It was indeed Elias who had caught his friend. He had Albrecht, with his tangle of brown curls, pressed up against the trunk of a tree, his own hands on either side of Albrecht's shoulders, trapping him. It was what Elias was doing that rooted Elisabeth to the spot. He leaned slowly forward, bringing his face down to the smiling Albrecht's, and he kissed him. Kissed him! He kissed him on the mouth, and Albrecht responded. He reached up his own arms, put them around Elias's body, and they melted together in an embrace that communicated itself somehow right to Elisabeth's belly.

Taking one step backward at a time, Elisabeth put the coppice between herself and the boys. Conflicting impulses assailed her. She wanted to turn and run all the way back to the manor. She wanted to burst in on them and demand an explanation. She followed another impulse instead, walking quietly to a spot by the brook, where she sat on her favorite boulder. Drawing up her knees, she wrapped her arms around her legs and dropped her chin to rest on them.

What were Elias and Albrecht doing?

She knew perfectly well what. She just had not realized boys would do that with each other.

She and Elias had been inseparable until three years ago, when Albrecht von Langenzenn had come to Winterkirche from his own family's manor to become a knight-in-training as Sigismund of Winterkirche's squire. It was then, Elisabeth now realized, that the bond between her and Elias had loosened. Though the three children were friends, she became aware of a special new bond between the boys. She'd complained to her mother about it. Adalberta had stroked her soft brown hair and assured her that Elias was of an age where he needed companions of his own sex. A pouting Elisabeth had nevertheless said nothing to her brother about feeling abandoned.

Sitting on the rock, Elisabeth stared unseeing at the brook as it flowed, tumbling over fallen branches and the stones of its streambed. Should she tell Mother about what she saw? Her innate loyalty to her twin above all others caused her to say "No!" aloud to the brook, the trees, and the birds around her. But wasn't it a sin? Were you not supposed to get married before you kissed anyone like that, and if so, how could two boys get married? She had never heard of such a thing. Should she say something to Elias himself? He would explain it to her. He was so kind and so wise. He would make it all right.

A shrill blast of a horn made Elisabeth look up, and she turned her head toward the manor. Father! It was Father, back from his journey to see Emperor Henry. She leaped to her feet and ran nearly to where she had spied on the two squires. Though she could not see the boys, she could hear giggling and shouted, "Elias! Father is home!"

Not waiting for her brother and his friend to join her, she turned and dashed back toward the walled compound that encircled her father's estate. Normally she would have made for an open wicket in the gate, but the two halves of the stout wooden barrier stood wide open now that the horses and men were trailing in. She slipped by the last stragglers into the courtyard. It was indeed her father, just now walking his horse to where grooms stood ready to take the reins. Mother stood in the doorway to the hall, offering her tired smile for her beloved husband.

"Papa! Papa!" Elisabeth cried, dashing up to join Sigismund as, dismounting, he went to Adalberta and returned her smile. He turned his head to see Elisabeth at his elbow. "Liebchen, darling, look at you. Every time I see you, you are taller! And prettier!"

He threw one arm around her shoulders and the other around his wife's. "Where is Elias?" he asked, drawing both of them up the stone steps to the hall.

"He's coming," Elisabeth replied, the excitement of her father's return banishing any other thoughts from her mind.

Sigismund did not seem to hear her reply, speaking excitedly to Adalberta as they entered the high-raftered room.

"His name is Peter the Hermit, a priest from Amiens, my dear, and I cannot wait to tell you what he said."

"Child!" It was the serving woman, Marta, who appeared and beckoned to Elisabeth. "For shame, to greet your lord father with your gown all in a mess! Come here!"

Elisabeth stopped and shook her head. "But...," she protested.

"You have plenty of time to hear your father's news, whatever it may be. Do you not want to look your best for him? I mean, look at your mother, so lovely, so groomed. You look like a cotter's brat."

Letting the woman draw her away, Elisabeth looked back at her parents. Indeed, Adalberta was lovely. Wan and sickly as she was, she nevertheless was dressed immaculately and glowed with pleasure as she went to the table by the fire, her arm tucked in her husband's.

A movement nearer the door caught Elisabeth's attention. "Marta, look at Elias. He is all over leaves and sticks and mud. Why do you not chastise him?"

"He's a boy. He is supposed to roughhouse. Now come."

Elisabeth sulked. There it was again. How she wished she were a boy.

Scrubbed, dressed in a more grown-up gown, her braids brushed and plaited again and coiled on either side of her head, Elisabeth was finally permitted to join her parents in the hall. Her sulk disappeared when, seeing her, Sigismund called out, "Darling girl!" He stood and bent, his arms out to enfold her in his embrace. When she stopped before him, he had to straighten up. "I said it before. You are getting so tall! Tall as your brother, I'll warrant. Here, Elias, come stand here by your sister. Yes, look at this, my wife. They are almost of a height."

The twins stood before their father. Elias was a respectable height for a boy of fifteen, but Elisabeth, hardly any shorter, was overtall for a girl. They couldn't, of course, be identical twins, but to look at them one would say they might as well be. Elias's hair, the exact color as his sister's, a light brown, was cropped while hers was coiled in braids. Their dark-brown eyes and rich eyelashes were the same. Their noses were small, too small for a boy, just right for a girl, and both had high, sculpted cheekbones and large, square jaws. Elisabeth saw that Elias was starting to show some fuzz on his chin, and she was green with envy.

"Now, you two, come sit with your mother and me. You as well, Albrecht. This concerns you too." Sigismund returned to his chair next to Adalberta. The three young people took seats usually reserved for guests. Elias and Albrecht normally served at table, being squires, and Elisabeth stood behind her mother during meals to see to her needs.

"His Holiness has had a plea from the Byzantine Emperor Alexios," Father was saying. "There have been attacks on pilgrims to the Holy Land, hundreds killed, hundreds carried off to the slave markets. The paynim no longer protect the pilgrimage routes, but let brigands have a free hand. There are rumors that some of the Turk leaders are sending their own guards to attack larger bands of pilgrims."

Adalberta put her hand to her lips. "No, how horrible. Why?"

The three young people turned their eyes back to Sigismund in unison.

"Well, there have always been brigands, but they have attacked randomly. Pilgrim bands that hired armed men to protect them could turn brigands away. No one really knows why that has changed, but Peter the Hermit said—"

Elias interrupted his father. "Peter the Hermit?" Elisabeth noted, not for the first time, how deep his voice had become.

"A French priest. He is in Cologne to gather pilgrims for a journey to the Holy Sepulchre in Jerusalem," Sigismund said.

"Not much of a hermit, is he?" Elias quipped, earning a short laugh from Elisabeth and a glare from both parents.

"Show some respect," Adalberta corrected. "He is a very holy man."

Sigismund took a gulp of the wine a servant had brought. His men, having seen to the disposition of their horses, were wandering into the hall and taking seats or leaning up against the timber walls to listen to their lord's account of the hermit's tale.

"He tried to make a pilgrimage to Jerusalem before, but he was captured by the Seljuk Turks in Anatolia and tortured."

Adalberta's eyes grew round.

"Why?" asked Elisabeth.

Sigismund sat forward, shaking his head. "They are heathens. They are devils. Cruel and rapacious. They are the enemy of all good Christians."

"But a priest!" Adalberta cried, unbelieving.

Albrecht shyly spoke up. "Mayhap they are even more violent with our holy men?"

The knight nodded. "It would seem so, lad."

Adalberta's eyes were guarded as she asked, "And this Peter… from Amiens, you say? He is gathering a multitude? To do what, my lord?"

"To return to the Holy Land and take Jerusalem back."

"He is gathering an army?" Elias's voice held a note of excitement. Elisabeth cast an alarmed look in his direction. Elias had been itching to be in a fight. He was disappointed when their father had failed to take him and Albrecht to Cologne for the meeting with the emperor's representatives. Both boys hoped the meeting was to plan war.

"No, not exactly," Sigismund replied, noting Elias's crestfallen reaction. "He is calling it a People's Crusade. Just the poor, the destitute who are under the care of Holy Church. But to hear him speak! It was inspiring. He said, 'Deus lo volt.' God wills it. We could not help but shout it back to him, every one of us in the throng."

Elias leaned to Albrecht and whispered, "I would wager the local bishops would not be sorry to see their burden thus eased—"

"Elias!" Sigismund's eyes were flaming. "Enough with your impious comments!" He glared at his chastened son, then slowly turned his face back to his wife. "Liebchen, I am going."

Adalberta hid her dismay. "I thought you might" was all she said.

"Then it is not just peasants going?" Elisabeth asked.

Her father sat up straight, squaring his shoulders. "They will need protection. Many of the emperor's commanders and officers are asking for leave to go with them." He looked sharply back at Adalberta. "I shall not go, if you are ill and need me here." His eyes revealed his reluctance to make such a promise. In a gentle voice meant only for her ears, he added, "But it is in large part to kneel at the Sepulchre and pray for your health and long life that I wish to go."

Before she could reply, Elias burst out, "Then Albrecht and I are coming with you?" He beamed at his friend, who returned the smile, but with anxiety written on his face.

Elisabeth looked from her father to brother to Albrecht and back again. A glance at her mother's averted face told her

Adalberta would not hold her husband back, no matter her misgivings. Tentatively, Elisabeth said, "Mother has been very weak of late."

"Nonsense, girl. It's just the season. You know how tired I get in the winter." Adalberta shook her head almost imperceptibly at her, as if begging her not to say more. "It is March. With the spring I will grow strong again."

Elisabeth continued to watch as the men talked excitedly of their upcoming adventure. She knew her mother, Adalberta del Luzio of Lombardy had never been strong, and had heard it said that giving birth to twins had weakened her further. The children, as they grew, were used to a mother who did not stir much from the manor, staying quiet and taking to her bed often. The twins were each other's support, as Sigismund was often away in one of the Holy Roman emperor's frequent wrangling battles with the pope. Elisabeth spent all the time she could with her brother, playing at boys' games, begging him to impart all he learned from his weapons master when they were old enough for Elias to be trained. Their mother tried to teach her the feminine art of needlework and instruct her in seemly comportment, but the moment the ailing woman took to her chambers, Elisabeth was out like a shot, looking for her twin and diligently mastering every masculine skill he gained.

They were accustomed to their mother's retiring life, but Elisabeth thought her mother had become paler of late. She had frequent debilitating headaches. Her joints were swollen and tender. During the occasional periods when Sigismund was not off serving his emperor, Adalberta masqueraded as best she could.

Looking at her now, Elisabeth could see she was lagging. Adalberta leaned to whisper in Sigismund's ear. He looked at her sharply, a smile lifting the corners of his lips. "Are you sure? Are you well enough?"

Adalberta deftly feigned enthusiasm. "I am, my lord, and it has been some time."

Sigismund grinned delightedly. To the company in the hall, he proclaimed, "I and my lady are tired and wish to seek our bed for a nap." He looked down when a few suggestive comments came from his men. "My love, go on up to our chamber. I would speak with our daughter." He kissed his wife on the cheek as she rose and then made her way to the stairs.

He watched Adalberta's retreating figure, then gestured to Elisabeth. "My dear, I have some excellent tidings for you. Come with me."

Elisabeth was already focused on her father, wondering what it was he had to tell her. Now she stood, exchanged puzzled looks with her twin brother, and followed their father to where he stopped near the foot of the stairs Adalberta had mounted. "Yes, Papa?" she asked.

Sigismund hesitated, then addressed her. "Liebchen, you are almost sixteen now, a woman. Your mother and I have neglected plans for your future."

Elisabeth eyed him warily.

"I have betrothed you to a fine man, a Freiherr of the duke of Bavaria. I think you know him."

Elisabeth's face went white. "Oh no, Papa, please! I do not wish to marry."

Sigismund looked sternly into Elisabeth's eyes. "But you must. Unless, of course, you wish to take the veil. I did not think so," he went on when she recoiled at the suggestion. "You will need a home and children like any other woman, and I have chosen a man of noble blood and excellent reputation who will provide for you and protect you."

Elisabeth stared, unbelieving. "Wh-who?"

"The Baron Reinhardt von Linkshändig. You remember some years ago when he came here?"

"B-but I thought he was married!" she stammered.

Sigismund put an arm around her and looked at the rushes on the floor. "He was. He lost his wife in childbed. Actually, both of his wives. He is twice a widower." He raised his head to look compassionately into her eyes. "My darling, he is a good man, a great knight, and loyal subject of the emperor. He is going on the pilgrimage with me. Now promise you will think about this, pray about it, and see the wisdom in it. Your brother will marry, and his wife will not want a spinster sister about. And you will want a household of your own. You know that's true."

Elisabeth nodded dumbly. "Yes, Papa."

"You will be married before we set out."

To Elisabeth, his words sounded like a death knell.

THE HOUSEHOLD plunged into activity at once. Despite anxiety for Adalberta, Sigismund could not hide his anticipation. Elias and Albrecht did not even try.

Elisabeth found herself left out of the boys' preparations. She could only stand on the periphery and watch glumly as the three men in her life spent every waking moment arranging to leave her behind, to a fate she could not comprehend. She realized how much more her mother must dread this parting. Though they had rarely talked, mother to daughter, Elisabeth sought Adalberta out and confided her fears.

"Mama, how will we bear it?" she sighed while the two sat together in Adalberta's solar.

Adalberta put a comforting hand on her daughter's supple one. "That is our lot, my dear. Women wait while men go abroad."

"Men are so selfish!" Elisabeth could not restrain her outburst.

Her mother shook her head. "Nay, it is not selfishness. It is duty. Theirs is to obey their masters. Ours is to obey them."

"I don't understand why it has to be like that. Peasant men and women work together in almost everything. I have seen them, side by side in the fields, planting or harvesting. Why can we not do the same? And why do they have to go to war anyway? It seems to me that life would be so much better without going to war." Elisabeth's face held a petulant sort of challenge.

Her mother finally prodded, "What else bothers you, my daughter?"

Elisabeth raised bleak eyes to her mother's face. With a hushed voice, she asked her, "Mama, do you think since Elias and I are twins, I might be more like him than if I had been born separately?"

Adalberta's frowned, her forehead furrowing. "What do you mean?"

"I mean, what if I am not entirely a girl? What if being twins means Elias and I share some of each other's, um, manliness and womanliness?"

"What in the Virgin's name are you talking about?" her mother said querulously.

Elisabeth would not meet her eyes. She did not share her thoughts about her brother's "unmanly" love for his friend. She was uncertain how to describe her own feelings of being in the wrong body. "I don't know. I just don't feel like a girl. I don't want anything of a woman's life. I don't enjoy sitting and sewing and waiting for the men to do all the living. I want to live too. I want what boys have."

Sighing, her mother shook her head. "I have failed you, my daughter, and for that I am most heartily sorry. I have not spent the time with you that I should. You spend all your time in your brother's company, never learning what it is to be a woman. I hoped Marta would fill my place, but she is even more indulgent than I." Reaching to cradle Elisabeth's chin in her palm, she drew Elisabeth's reluctant eyes to her own. "Perhaps it is best if my lord does go to the Holy Land and prays for my health. Perhaps it is not too late for me to spend the time with you I have neglected. There is so much you have to learn before you are wed."

Fear clouded Elisabeth's eyes. "And that is another thing! I hardly know Reinhardt. What I do remember, I did not like."

"He is strong and can provide for you and your children. He is an honorable man you can be proud of." She let go of Elisabeth's chin. "It is for the best."

Elisabeth stood and stepped stiffly to the window embrasure. "I shan't need to be provided for. I will die giving birth to his brats just like his other wives. That's all women are for. To have babies, then die." Her thoughtless words hit her like a slap. She whirled to face her mother. "Oh, my dearest Mama, I am so sorry! I did not mean...."

Adalberta shook her head compassionately. "I know you did not mean to hurt my feelings. And truly, darling, I understand your fear. You cannot know the joys that make it all worthwhile. The companionship of your husband, the satisfaction of running your household, and, most of all, the love for your children." She put out her thin arms to Elisabeth, who went to her, knelt, and leaned into the embrace.

"You have Papa. He loves you. That is why you endure it all."

Pressing Elisabeth's head to her breast, Adalberta reassured her, "Your Papa and I love each other very much, and it is true. But we did not even know each other when we were wed. Love came over time. And from our union came you and your brother. Just think, if I had thought like you do now, none of that could have ever come about."

Elisabeth nodded against her mother's body. "I don't understand how Papa can go and leave you suffering."

"It is because I am suffering that he is going!"

Looking up at her mother's strained expression, Elisabeth shook her head. "I know that, Mama, but it is more. He wants to go. Almost as much as Elias and Albrecht. Why do they want to go and leave us behind?"

Adalberta pulled Elisabeth up so she could sit beside her on the settle. Putting her arm around Elisabeth's waist, she chuckled. "I think you know why the boys want to go. As for your father…." She paused. "Let me see if I can explain it. Your father was ever a loyal man to Emperor Henry, in spite of the great man's petty quarrels with the Holy Father. Over the years, he has become disillusioned. He says that he now believes that the emperor has used the disputes simply for his own arrogant purposes." She leaned her head on Elisabeth's. "You know your father is a brave and honorable knight. He needs to turn his energies to a worthy cause. He needs… redemption."

Elisabeth subsided. "I know, Mama. But I will miss them all. And I will worry as well."

"As will I, dearest. As will I." She lifted her head and leaned to look into Elisabeth's face. "But think of it, liebchen, we have a wedding to plan! Is that not exciting too?"

Without conviction Elisabeth answered, "Yes, Mama."

Also from Harmony Ink Press

BREAKING
FREE

WINTER PAGE

www.harmonyinkpress.com

FOR MORE OF THE BEST

TEEN & NEW ADULT FICTION

Harmony Ink

VISIT

HARMONYINKPRESS.COM